D1042141

the
fruit bowl
project

a novel by

SARAH DURKEE

delacorte press

Published by Delacorte Press, an imprint of Random House Children's Books
a division of Random House, Inc., New York

Visit us on the Web! www.randomhouse.com/teens
Educators and librarians, for a variety of teaching tools,
visit us at www.randomhouse.com/teachers

Library of Congress Cataloging-in-Publication Data
Durkee, Sarah.
The Fruit Bowl Project / Sarah Durkee.
p. cm.
Summary: An admittedly "dork" middle-school teacher arranges for a rock superstar to
teach her eighth-grade students, who each tell a story about the same topic, in the style of
a rap, poem, monologue, screenplay, haiku, fairytale, and more.
ISBN 0-385-73289-9 (trade)—ISBN 0-385-90310-3 (Gibraltar lib. bdg.)
[1. Teachers—Fiction. 2. Musicians—Fiction. 3. Rock music—Fiction. 4. Middle
schools—Fiction. 5. Schools—Fiction. 6. Creative writing—Fiction.] I. Title.
PZ7.D934247Fru 2006
[Fic]—dc22
2005003908

The text of this book is set in 12-point Adobe Caslon.

Book design by Kayley LeFaiver

Printed in the United States of America

January 2006

10 9 8 7 6 5 4 3 2 1

BVG

For Ruby and Charlie,
lurve you beyond words.

Acknowledgments

Thanks to all the great kids and brilliant teachers at the Manhattan New School, the Center School, and the Ethical Culture Fieldston School for being endlessly inspiring.

Deepest thanks to Beverly Horowitz for seeing the Big Canvas way before I did, and making this a better book than I'd ever dreamt it could be.

Thanks and much love to Paul Jacobs, Kevin Wade, Carolyn Swartz, Ryan Wojtanowski, and Timothy Holst for their eyes and ears and cheers and great advice.

Thanks to Sophie Hicks for being so breathtakingly fleet of brain and foot, not to mention darn fun.

And humble acknowledgment to Raymond Queneau, whose *Exercises in Style* provided the lightbulb.

No one ever thought of Ms. Vallis as being particularly hip. But she was the newest teacher at West Side Middle, which gave her a certain freshness factor, and her enthusiasm hadn't been pounded out of her by too many years of Eighth-Grade Attitude yet. She was even known to stick up for this or that kid with *very* bad attitude, in that way of petite female teachers who are secretly thrilled that someone who probably would've smashed them into a locker back when they were thirteen now actually needs them. (Lion, mouse, thorn, paw.) Her dark hair was unfussy and longish, and she was an admitted "dork," which helped the kids suspect she really wasn't, and she taught the eighth-grade Lit class and Writers' Workshop.

On this hot September morning, when the sun was still taunting everybody that it was summer somewhere, her 8:45 class sat like caged puppies.

"Good morning, happy young people!" Ms. Vallis sing-songed. Seb Harris groaned from the back of the room, his shaggy head in his arms. Katie Parker, Jenna Bromberg, and

Emily McGee did their usual jokey, suck-uppy echo of "Good morniiiiing, Ms. Valliiiiiiiis!" Their skirts were all extremely short, all the color of breath mints, all expensive.

"Who wants good news?" Ms. Vallis teased. "Who wants *great* news?"

"Me," Rob Bellevance said morosely. "The Yankees are sucking."

"Go, Mets!" shouted Fish Koenig, jabbing his fist.

"Mets bite!" Amir Azzam threw in.

"Gee, guess what, guys? It's *not about sports*! " she continued.

"Yay," said Jenna, eye-rolling.

"Thank God," said Katie.

"Thank GOD," agreed Emily.

"Shut UP!" growled Pearl Richardson, the Girl in Black. All obeyed the Girl in Black. Pearl was beautiful, with lunar skin and long coppery hair and a flair for dark comments that made Daria look almost perky. But anyone calling Pearl "goth" was met with fury, because she hated categories.

"It's about my cousin's husband," Ms. Vallis announced. Incomplete, attention-grabbing statements were her specialty.

Jenna yelped "Woo!" knowingly. Everyone else waited.

"*I* know who he is," said Jenna, "but I didn't wanna tell everybody because my mom said you probably want to respect his privacy."

"Except she did tell me and Katie and Carly," Emily clarified. "But we didn't tell anybody either."

"Thanks," said Ms. Vallis. "I so appreciate that. But it's

okay, this is a good time to tell everybody. Go ahead, Jenna. Tell everybody who my cousin's husband is."

Jenna paused for dramatic effect. This was how she tended to say nearly everything, as in, "She was wearing a *bathing suit* with . . ." pause . . . *"UGG BOOTS!"* But this time the drama was extreme even for Jenna. Her eyes looked like a huge close-up in a mascara ad.

"Her cousin . . . is married . . . to *NICK THOMPSON!"*

The room exploded with a mixture of appreciative whoops and demands for explanation. Most people knew who Nick Thompson was—he was too famous to miss—but a few kids who were new to the U.S. or who were rock-'n'-roll-and-TV-deprived weren't quite sure.

"Nick Thompson is a musical *icon!*" raved Katie. "He's a *god!*"

"Well, I think he'd be quick to dismiss the god comparison," Ms. Vallis smiled.

"He's right up there with Steven Tyler!" exclaimed Fish.

"Who's Steven Tyler?" said Yun Li.

"Liv Tyler's dad," Emily said helpfully.

"Who's Liv Tyler?"

Yun was widely thought to be the coolest kid in school because he didn't care even slightly about being cool. His cello case had been duct-taped together, not in a cool way but by necessity, until Mr. Holst, the part-time music teacher, bought him a new one with his own money.

"Okay," Fish tried again, "Nick Thompson is practically as famous as Bob Dylan."

Yun shrugged. "Don't know him either."

Ms. Vallis, to everyone's acute distress, took this as her cue to start swaying and singing "Blowin' in the Wind" in a folky PBS voice. Yun's eyes lit up with awestruck recognition.

"Your cousin's husband wrote 'Blowin' in the Wind'?"

She looked a little deflated. "No."

"Oh," said Yun.

Everyone burst out laughing, even Ms. Vallis. She screwed up her face, reached back into the seventies, and rattled off a list. "But he did write 'Plastic Soldiers'. . . 'Gimme Strength'. . . 'My Very High Priestess'. . ."

Corey Lewis couldn't resist singing "My Very High Priestess" in Nick Thompson's famous growl:

> *"Mah very high priestess*
> *High priestess of quirks*
> *She opens your mind*
> *Just to see how it works*
> *Assesses your messes*
> *and blesses your soul*
> *Then climbs to her throne*
> *While you crawl in a hole—"*

Tionna Chapman cut him off. "That song is wack. I always hated that song. And it makes no sense."

"It's poetry, Tionna," said Jenna condescendingly. "It doesn't have to make sense."

4

"It's rock!" said Fish. "It doesn't have to . . . *anything*."

"It's cool but it ain't rap, dawg," said David Edelman. David had come back to school this year trying so hard to be gangsta, he'd even convinced his dentist father to make him a gold tooth.

"And you can't dance to it! Gimme hip-hop any day," chimed Tionna.

"I'm down witcha, girl," David nodded his do-rag.

"But he's a genius! I bet 'high' is a drug reference. I didn't get that when I was little but it's, like, soooo obvious now," chirped Emily.

"Ohmigod, definitely, like 'Lucy in the Sky with Diamonds'!" added Jenna.

Pearl moaned and squished her pale face between her hands. "Can we please hear the great news before I twist my own head off and run screaming from the room?"

"Okay," Ms. Vallis refereed. She sat on the edge of her desk in a failed effort to look casual. Her anchorwoman hornrims were meant to give her round young face some gravity, but no one was fooled. She was always prone to plain old cheesy youthful excitement, even about certain passages of *Tortilla Flats*. Now her excitement was popping off her like sparks. How often does a teacher get to set the dogs loose?

She took a deep breath.

"He's visiting tomorrow. Here. Nick Thompson is coming to your Writers' Workshop."

These kids were not easy to impress. They were sophisticated New York City kids, pretty used to spotting celebrities

5

in their midst. Jerry Seinfeld at Starbucks. Gwyneth Paltrow in the park with Apple. Mary-Kate and Ashley all over the place. But . . . Nick Thompson? Coming to their school?? Ms. Vallis's Lit class went nuts.

▼　●　▲

He was coming to talk to them about *writing*. Everyone hung out in the hallway the following morning pondering this. It would be one thing, some kids pointed out, if this were some kind of Career Day talk. Or a commencement speech, where sometimes famous people get roped into talking to the graduating class. Fish said his dad's class had Paul Newman. Which prompted Belinda Voskidis to wonder why in the world they'd pick "some guy who makes popcorn! Bizarre!" but when they stopped guffawing they filled her in on the rest of his career.

West Side Middle was small enough so that every single kid in school had heard about Nick Thompson's visit by first period. Ms. Vallis had tried not to make too big a deal out of it, to keep it from becoming a "carnival-like atmosphere," as she put it. But please. Nick Thompson! Kids and even teachers kept lurking around room 324, some not even bothering to hide their crazed-fan status. Everyone acted like they had an extremely important stapler to borrow, or sauntered in to retrieve conveniently forgotten notebooks. Ms. Vallis shooed them all away as the time for her eleven-thirty Writers' Workshop approached, with the promise that if all went well, they might be able to make it a tradition for future eighth grades.

"Yeah, right," snorted Seb. "I'm sure Nick Thompson will be making this a regular gig."

At 11:26 they were all in their seats. Ms. Vallis was wearing her idea of a very edgy outfit, which was kind of heartbreaking to the girls who cared about such things (black pants, T-shirt, *leopard belt*). She assured the class he'd be there any minute; he'd just called from his car to say he'd stopped to get a triple-shot grande latte for the "caffeine-fueled approximation of consciousness." This direct quote warmed everybody up, and they chattered among themselves in a friendlier way than usual, each with one eye glued to the door.

His voice entered first. "I haven't been in a junior high since 1964!" he crowed from the hallway. "Is this it? Three twenty-four? Ritaaaaa! Lovely Ritaaaa. . . !"

Nothing had quite prepared them for the three-dimensional experience of Nick Thompson. He came into the room like a kinetic sculpture, like a broken accordion, like tin cans and balloons tied to the back of a car. He gave "Rita" a bear hug, actually lifting her off her feet with her edgy little black boots dangling, and she giggled like she was twelve before she remembered she was an authority figure.

"G'morning, tortured pawns of the New York City school system!" his sandpaper voice greeted them. They laughed, sort of. He pulled a chair next to Ms. Vallis, turned it backward, and straddled it as any self-respecting Rock Icon would do. "Thanks for givin' me a reason to get outa bed!"

He cackled merrily, then quickly transitioned into a scary hacking cough that went on for so long the kids had plenty of time to take him in.

He was old, by their math, and in natural light he looked it. His wrinkled face bore the indentations of every tour bus window, airplane seat belt, backstage ashtray, and flying mike stand of the past thirty-five years, and maybe a few fists. His hair was a long reddish brown tangle, and his clothes were the kind of Technicolor pirate rags found only in stores frequented by skinny rock stars and their offspring. A pair of Hello Kitty sunglasses was hanging from his shirt pocket, which everyone in the room immediately embraced as the coolest, most uniquely macho accessory they'd ever seen.

Oh, and he had a nicotine patch on his forearm, upon which someone had drawn a burning cigarette.

He was fantastic.

"I guess I don't need to make a formal introduction, but . . ." Ms. Vallis gestured broadly like a TV show hostess presenting prizes. "Nick Thompson . . . the West Side Middle School eighth-grade Writers' Workshop!"

Everyone burst into applause and whistles.

"Thanks, guys," he said, smiling. "I'm glad to be here."

He suddenly looked almost shy, jiggling his knees. Everybody was struck dumb by the surreal familiarity of his famous face.

"I guess I should tell you how Nick and I came up with the idea for this visit," Ms. Vallis continued. "We were at my cousin's fiftieth-birthday party—"

"The old bag!" he growled playfully.

"—and we started talking about writing as a craft," she continued, ignoring him. "And I said, 'How do you feel about *your* writing?'"

"And I said, 'Pretty crappy, generally!'" he said, laughing.

The kids chuckled dutifully. They knew this couldn't possibly be true; the man had written dozens of hit songs, timeless classics.

"No, I mean it!" he insisted. "Ninety percent of what I write is total . . . hamster droppings," he said, checking himself with a smile. "Garbage."

Katie raised her hand and started talking before she was even called on. This was typical, the birthright of the Effortlessly Popular.

"How do you get your ideas?" she asked brightly. Of all the questions to ask a visiting artist, this was probably the most common, and everyone else in the room vowed to do better if they got the chance.

"Substance abuse," he said gravely. "Massive quantities of drugs."

This was quite an icebreaker. The room erupted with shrieks of laughter. Ms. Vallis scolded him vigorously and attempted to restore order. Seb Harris, in particular, would not stop howling.

"Quiet!" snapped Greta Stern. "Some of us would actually like to hear!" Greta was the biggest grade-grubber in the eighth grade, and so aptly named Stern it was hard to believe.

"We've all seen *Behind the Music*," Ms. Vallis teased, "so we all know the drug stuff hasn't been true for a looooong time.

And we all admire that tremendously," she added primly. "But here's what I'd really, really like to talk about today, Nick. When you sit down to write, just as everyone in this class sits down to write . . . what is it that makes a Nick Thompson song a Nick Thompson song? When I asked you that at the party, you said something very interesting. You said" —and here she enunciated professorially and held her finger in the air— "'A song's just a bowl of fruit, and I've just gotta figure out how to paint it.'"

"Ooooh, did I say that?" he joked. "I *like* that."

"Yes, you said that," she replied with a laugh. "I like it too. I want you to elaborate, and then you have an assignment for us. So . . . Nick, you have the floor!"

She walked to a desk off to the side, sat herself down comfortably, and crossed her arms.

"O-kaaaay," Nick began, standing. "Ooooo-kay—"

"Do you still have groupies?" Seb interrupted loudly.

"Yeah," Nick replied. "I have to scrape them off the windshield every morning like *snow*, man. Now, as I was saying—"

"Do you tour?" Seb persisted.

"*Seb!*" Ms. Vallis barked.

Nick's smile was getting a little crooked. He sat down again, gathered his thoughts, and then shot a level gaze at Seb. "The thing is, what's cool about coming here is that I like kids to understand something about the Rock Star thing. And that's that it's not all crazy, it's not all the big concerts and partying at the hotel and marrying fashion models thing. Unfortunately."

Chuckles.

"What it is, for many, many hours of my life, is me in my total nerd reading glasses, all alone. A massive nerd with a pen and a spiral notebook, trying to think of the right word and feeling like a total champ when I find it. Like it is for anybody trying to write anything. Whether it's rock songs or love letters or cereal boxes."

There was a semirespectful silence.

"Oh my GOD was that profound!" he screamed, jumping to his feet again. The kids were back in the palm of his hand.

"Okay, let's continue. 'A song is like a bowl of fruit.' Let's start with that. What do you think I meant by that?"

"That it's . . . fruity?" said Rob tentatively.

Laughter, of course. Eighth grade.

"Yes, I mean my songs are *fruity*," Nick deadpanned over the laughter. "My songs are completely homosexual."

"Watch it," said Brendan Torres, his eyes narrowed.

"His brother's gay," clarified Emily.

"Cool. So's my manager, and I think my cat," Nick said. The laughter chuckled down comfortably. "Moving right along, here's what I mean. My theory is that for a writer, every song, or every story, that they sit down to write is just like a bowl of fruit that a painter sets out to paint. And every bowl of fruit is different. Then comes the good part. How many ways do you think there are to paint that simple bowl of fruit?"

"A million?" said someone.

"Probably infinite," mumbled Pearl.

"Infinite!" repeated Nick. "Let's go with infinite. Because it's probably true, right? There are an *infinite* number of ways to paint it, depending on who's painting it and how they want it to look. Every choice of color, shadow, texture, line . . . I ain't no art teacher, but you get the drift." He laughed and glanced at Ms. Vallis for approval.

She nodded and smiled. "Keep going, you're on a roll."

"Okay, um—"

"Will we be painting?" Jazzmyn Rivera interrupted hopefully. She was an artist and anime freak.

Ms. Vallis was patient. "He's making an *analogy*, Jazzmyn. That writing is like painting."

"Because," Nick jumped in, "words are to a writer what paint is to a painter, right? They're your colors! So when I sit down to write a song about, say, a rainy night, a dark-haired girl, and a phone call . . . how many ways can I tell that story? That particular bowl of fruit? I have the whooooole language at my fingertips, right? The whooooole spectrum of color."

"Lemme guess. . . an infinite number of ways?" teased Fish.

"Bingo! Infinite!"

Nick was definitely warmed up.

"So what's the assignment?" Greta pressed. "What are we writing, and when is it due?"

"Let me jump in for just one second," Ms. Vallis said, "and add to Nick's point. What is it we're talking about when we talk about color in writing?"

"Style?" said Katie.

"Yes."

"Genre?" said Amir.

"Yes!"

"Voice?" said Tionna.

"Right!" said Ms. Vallis. She looked positively pink-cheeked with the wonderfulness of her students. The fluorescent lights hummed. Nick was writing something on the blackboard, clacking away with the chalk furiously. The class sat back in that pleasant stupor of students who will momentarily be told what to do. It was remarkable. In a mere ten minutes, a rock god had turned from a giddy fantasy into a flesh-and-blood guy they could see, and hear, and stop paying attention to.

"Do you have, like, a huge crib?" David drawled.

"Yeah," answered Nick as he chalked.

"*Writing*, David," Ms. Vallis snapped. "This is about writing, not his 'crib.'"

Nick turned back to the class, eyes sparkling, revved. On the blackboard was scrawled the following:

BOWL OF FRUIT = THE IMMUTABLE TRUTH

"Okay, now for your assignment. First let's decide what our story is, cuz you're all gonna write the saaaaame one. The same fruit bowl. Or what I like to call the Immutable Truth! Like that? I just made that up right this second." He was as excited as a little kid. They couldn't help getting caught up in his personal party.

He asked for story ideas. Brendan suggested a shark attack. "A shark bites that surfer chick's *other* arm off."

"You're a sick man," clucked Nick. "Gimme less."

"A kidnapping?" ventured Katie. "Something to do with a kidnapping?"

"Maybe . . ."

Fish could always be counted on for creativity. "An Arab and a Jew are stuck in an elevator during a blackout?"

"Very cool!" Nick enthused. "But are you ready? Here's your story. Name the most boring, normal place you can think of."

"School," Pearl volunteered.

"Ouch!" said Ms. Vallis.

SCHOOL, Nick dutifully chalked on the board.

"Okay. Name a grade you've already been in. Because writing what you know about is always best."

"Sixth," offered Rob.

6TH GRADE, Nick wrote.

"Okay. Now we need a really typical school activity."

"A test," Greta called. "A reading test."

READING TEST, he wrote.

"Now the most ordinary thing that can happen during a reading test."

"Someone farts," offered Rob.

"Too exciting."

"Someone drops a pencil," said Yun.

"Perfect!"

DROPPED PENCIL, he wrote. "So let's add a little

drama—a kid drops a pencil and he bumps a girl's arm when he picks it up."

"Ooooh!" The class laughed. They were getting into the spirit of this ordinary-fruit-bowl concept.

"And it makes the girl make a mark on her test, and she's furious!" said Katie. She blushed, as if she might have some firsthand knowledge of this kind of thing.

GIRL MAD, wrote Nick.

"Okay, a little scene change. Name another school thing."

"Lunch," said Belinda.

LUNCH, he added.

"Something funny that happens at lunch," prompted Nick.

"Food fiiiiiight!" howled Corey Lewis.

"Hm. A little too *Animal House*," Nick cautioned. "We need ordinary."

"I got it. Somebody laughs so hard milk comes outa their nose," Tionna said. Everybody recognized perfection when they heard it.

MILK OUT THE NOSE, Nick scrawled on the board with a flourish.

"And there you have it! Your story!" he crowed.

The silence was deafening.

SCHOOL
6TH GRADE
READING TEST
DROPPED PENCIL

GIRL MAD
LUNCH
MILK OUT THE NOSE

—was all that appeared.

"That's all that happens?" Emily said skeptically.

"That's aaall the fruit in the bowl, folks. That's it. Because this assignment is about *style*. It ain't the story, it's *how you tell it* that counts. It's pretty easy to make a shark attack interesting. Your job is to make *this*" —he clacked the chalk on the list—"interesting. By telling it absolutely any way you want. Any style, any genre, any point of view."

"As a rap?" David muttered. Everybody tittered.

"*Sure* as a rap. Definitely!"

The energy in the room rose almost perceptibly, like a breeze before a rainstorm.

"As a screenplay?" asked Fish. His mother was a casting agent, and he was obsessed with movies.

"Absolutely!" Nick said. "As a poem, as a monologue . . . I don't wanna give you too many ideas, you'll come up with better stuff on your own. But no getting too creative with the Immutable Truth, got it? You've all got the exact same fruit bowl to paint. Let's sketch in some more apples and bananas. Who *are* these kids? The school is called . . ."

"I.S. 280," Ms. Vallis tossed in.

He wrote information down in a flurry of chalk as the kids spontaneously called it out.

Date:
April 20
Setting:
Very hot classroom
Time:
11:05 a.m.
Teacher:
Ms. Petricoff
Boy who drops pencil:
Kevin Marchetti (troublemaker)
Girl who gets mad:
Zoe Blass (very popular goody-goody)
Boy who tells joke:
Kevin Marchetti
Boy who spews drink out nose all over lunch:
Jason Allen (Kevin's sidekick, has secret crush on Zoe)
Lunch:
Chicken nuggets
Santa Fe potato skins
Chocolate milk
Ending:
They throw their lunches away

"That's really how it ends?" Greta fretted. "This is such a lame, pathetic story. No offense. But what's the point?"

Everyone looked at Nick, hoping for a far better explanation than they could offer.

"The point," he told them, beaming, "is to paint a damn good bowl of fruit!"

The man certainly was a performer. As if on cue, the ear-splitting lunch bell rang immediately after he uttered the word *fruit*. He did a spastic jump and clutched his chest in mock terror, which cracked everyone up.

"I'll be back in two weeks to see what you come up with, okay? Can't wait. Bye, Miz Valliiis." He kissed Ms. Vallis on the cheek. "Happy writing!"

And he was out the door.

The usual hallway chaos was a little more festive with Nick Thompson sightings as everyone scattered for lunch. Ms. Vallis's class was feeling very possessive of him by now, but they had to share him. Self-conscious laughter spilled out of the faculty room as he stopped in to say hi, and he was glimpsed through a partially open door thanking the principal, Ms. Waite, in her office. He pulled kids along like iron filings as he made his way out of the building and down to his car on the street, even signing a few autographs for anybody brave enough to ask. And with a roar of his hybrid engine (cool/not cool, the kids were divided), he was off, waving from the window.

▼　●　▲

Lunchtime at West Side Middle was a hierarchy. On the bottom rung were the sixth graders, who hadn't yet earned the right to leave the school without supervision for any reason. They all ate in the cafeteria along with the elementary school kids who shared the building, or they brought a slightly humiliating lunch from home. Seventh graders were a mixed bag of kids who ate in the cafeteria and kids who had written permission from their parents to leave the school grounds for lunch. Almost every eighth grader had permission to leave, which they did, in loud clusters of kids headed for very distinct territories.

Katie, Jenna, and Emily had lately been walking to a little Japanese specialty store a few blocks away. They would sit at a cafe table sipping bubble tea, their new favorite, and sharing sushi. Other girls would sit nearby, forming a larger category of Katie-Jenna-Emily knockoffs who fooled themselves into believing they were much more of a democracy and not as popular *by choice*. This worked well for everyone. They had all seen movies and TV shows about Mean Queens and Wannabes and they were very adamant that their school was *very* different, ohmigod completely.

Carly Heywood was the unofficial leader of these B-list girls. She'd moved from a suburban school to the city, which made her highly exotic, and she had an irrepressible cheerleader demeanor that the other girls made fun of but envied. Belinda Voskidis of the distracting body and sketchy brain, Cassie DiGiovanni of the nonstop mouth, and Jocelyn Higuchi completed the group. Jocelyn was so nice she was usually exhausted from the sheer effort of being everyone's closest friend.

The talk was about Nick Thompson, of course. Not all the girls had been in Ms. Vallis's Writers' Workshop.

"He was awesome," gushed Katie. "*So* funny. *So* cool."

"I'm actually excited about the assignment," said Belinda. "How often does *that* happen?"

"It's so incredibly unfair that only one class got to have him visit," complained Cassie, rubbing her chopsticks together. "Does anyone else want to talk to Ms. Vallis about that? About the unfairness of that? Not, like, the *unfairness,* but the jealousy? Not jealousy, but disappointment? Of everybody else?"

"You can just say 'unfairness,' Cassie." Jenna rolled her eyes.

"Want some of my California roll?" offered Jocelyn.

▼ ● ▲

Maeve Gillis, Sandra Bruce, and Rosie Ramos huddled over their pizza. They hadn't been in Ms. Vallis's class but had of course heard about it.

"That sucks," Rosie chewed. "*I* wanna get that Nick Thompson assignment. It sounds cool."

"Who's stopping you?" Maeve thumbed her iPod. "Ask Ms. Vallis in Lit today. You suck-up."

Sandra twiddled the earrings that studded the entire pink crescent of her left ear. "Should I love Nick Thompson?" she mused. "Does everyone in the world but me?"

▼ ● ▲

Seb Harris stomped his cigarette out when he saw Diz Cavallaro coming. Their mothers were friends. He nodded at her without the derision he usually aimed at her group. She was nice, a future teacher type.

"Hi," she murmured tightly. Tionna Chapman, Deena Prajapati, and Madeleine Beers hustled her away, and they jogged shrieking toward Burger King.

"He's brilliant, don't you think?" demanded Tionna when they'd snagged a table.

Diz looked incredulous. "Seb?"

"No, *Nick Thompson!*" cackled Tionna.

"He's so skinny it's scary," marveled Deena to Diz, who hadn't been there.

The girls had to shout over the volume of the boys eating nearby. Rob, Fish, Corey, David, and Amir were singing Thompson's "Plastic Soldiers" with air guitar for Jawshua Perry, who was not a fan.

"That is not a sound that black people can hear," he joked, shaking his head. "That is like a *dog* whistle to black people, man. That's white people's jump-up-and-down-in-a-stadium-cuz-you-dance-like-crap music."

"Yeah, well, I'm gonna write me a rap for the assignment," David crowed.

"I'd probably write sci-fi if it was my class," Jawshua said, "but I'm glad I don't gotta."

"Maybe you're gonna get the same assignment," Amir mumbled through french fries.

"Aw, maaaan," Jawshua whined, but he looked almost hopeful.

▼ ● ▲

There were too many other eighth graders out to lunch to mention them all. They pushed each other into mailboxes (Brendan Torres, Buddy Corsa). They yelled to each other across the street (Thai Wheeler, Milo Korzienowsky). They kissed each other in doorways (Ben Rizzo, Jessica Hochstein). They strode through the crowds and delis and glittering traffic of the neighborhood like royalty, like someone had just informed them that everything they beheld was their inheritance, because they were all finally thirteen.

The following is a short list of kids who ate at school:

>Stephanie Jones (free lunch program)
>Morgan Greenwald (too spacey to go out)
>Dakota Falk (too allergic to eat anything but spelt
>bread and soy cheese from home)
>A.J. Conway (too medicated)

The following is a list of kids who worked in classrooms instead of having lunch:

>Max Baum-White (preparing PowerPoint biology
>presentation)
>Gary Beemer (Latin help)
>Justin Sirk (updating school Web site)
>Danielle Nesby (joining heated policy discussion with
>principal and city-appointed parent liaison)

Greta Stern (AP math help)
Mia McCabe-Alvarez (painting banners for Field Day)

The following is a list of kids who were absent:

Jeff Reese (faking sick, never heard Nick Thompson
    was coming)
Jonathan Fleck-Fishman (strep test)
Marina Kolodzyn (stomachache)

And the following is a list of kids who were invisible:

Chardinay King
Cameron Haas
Steven Spivack

▼   ●   ▲

A fax from Nick Thompson came into the office the next
morning. Rob Bellavance and Thai Wheeler had faxed him
some questions, just to see if he'd answer, when so many kids
were mad they hadn't gotten a chance to meet him.

FAX
To: West Side Middle School
From: Nick Thompson
Sept. 16

Hi guys,

That was such a blast. If I go get a teaching degree, it's all your fault.

Here are the answers to your questions:

WHAT'S YOUR MIDDLE NAME?
Nick (Nicholas) is actually my middle name. My first name is Marcel. My mom was French. Guess how many times you get your ass kicked with the name Marcel?

WHAT'S YOUR FAVORITE PLACE YOU'VE EVER TOURED?
Reykjavik, Iceland. A weird steaming planet with beautiful blond girls. It's like an old *Star Trek* episode.

WHO'S YOUR FAVORITE POET?
Dylan Thomas.

WHAT'S YOUR FAVORITE BEATLES SONG?
"Ticket to Ride." Ringo kills. "She Said" for trippy

genius. "Penny Lane" for the happiest pop song of all time.

WHAT'S YOUR MOST CHERISHED POSSESSION?
My sobriety. (Honestly, Oprah! It really is.)

WHAT'S ON YOUR BEDSIDE TABLE?
Picture of my wife and kids, golf tees, nicotine gum, used Kleenex, unfinished novel written by friend.

WHAT DEAD PERSON WOULD YOU MOST LIKE TO HANG OUT WITH?
That fossilized chick they found who's the oldest human. I'd take her to the Museum of Natural History and she could critique the dioramas. Then I'd buy her a milk shake.

WHAT'S YOUR FAVORITE SONG YOU'VE EVER WRITTEN?
The one I sang to my kids when they had ear infections, called "Ow Ow Ow."

BOXERS OR BRIEFS?

I enjoy layering—first a
thong, then briefs, then boxers.

But . . . what you guys think
is waaaay more important than
what I think. So go think.
See you soon!

Love, Nick

Ms. Vallis read it to all of her classes, and it got passed around all day.

"He's so full of himself," sniffed Sandra in the afternoon Lit class. "I love these famous types who think we *care*, y'know? About their stupid quirky-funky pop-culture opinions. It's so narcissistic."

"But we *do* care! We *asked* him!" said Diz.

No one could take the fun out of something like Sandra could. But she was so wickedly smart everybody always hung on her every word. She was Asian and had a chip on her shoulder about what a cliché that was, and once said if she ever had kids she hoped they'd be incredibly stupid. She, Pearl, Jazzmyn, Rosie, and Maeve were the Artsy Girls, which meant they were antigroup, which meant they weren't really a group except in everyone else's minds.

Ms. Vallis was fielding a few questions about Nick Thompson and what had come to be known as the Fruit Bowl Project before they got down to a discussion about *I Know*

Why the Caged Bird Sings. The first piece of writing had already been turned in that morning, from Corey Lewis, who wasn't in this class. He always worked fast. Ms. Vallis had been thrilled with his originality. It was so short and sweet she'd scrawled it on the blackboard to inspire everybody.

LIMERICK
With thumbs that were barely prehensile
An oafish young lad flipped a pencil
When his nuggets got shot
With some chocolate milk snot
He cracked up like all sixth-grade gents'll.

"That's an okay way to tell it?" said Danielle. "That short?"

"Sure," said Ms. Vallis. "Absolutely anything is okay as long as it's appropriate for the style of writing you pick. Maybe it's a style where spelling and grammar aren't even important. These won't even be graded! The only important thing is that you have fun with them, and that you turn them in. There's no right or wrong way, just *your* way! Sorry some of you didn't get to be involved—"

"'Pencil/*gents'll*'?" sneered Graham Beckwith. "Isn't that a bit of a *stretch*?"

"C'mon, it's a cool limerick!" said Rosie. "It's funny!"

Everyone shook their heads, smiling, marveling at it. It just glowed up there on the blackboard, gloated almost. Saying, *Nyah nyah, beat this for cleverness.* It was so Corey. But it also opened up everyone's minds to a world of possibilities. How would they write the story if they felt like trying? If a goofy limerick was possible . . .

Maeve raised her hand. "So . . . can other people hand in stuff besides the kids in your Writers' Workshop?" she said, peering through smoky eyeliner.

"Yeah," Jawshua added casually. "I've got sort of an idea for it too. But not as short."

Ms. Vallis tried very hard to restrain an impulse to jump up on a desk and start dancing around, pumping her fist in the air.

"Sure!" She smiled. "All of you can. We'll make a book."

▼ ● ▲

Here are the notable things that happened over the next few days:

David Edelman swallowed his gold tooth in gym.
Jessica Hochstein broke up with Ben Rizzo.
Katie Parker cried over an unfair B+ on a social studies test.
Seb Harris and Buddy Corsa were caught shoplifting at Tower Records.

The police let them off with a warning. Everyone knew it was probably Seb's idea; Buddy was just a kid with no common sense. Seb and his mother emerged from Ms. Waite's office after school the next day in silence. His mother's eyes were red, and Seb stared at a point straight ahead, a flat, limp backpack slung low on his back. Even this had been a bone of contention between them this year.

"Look at that worthless backpack," she'd snarled midfight. "Are you *proud* of the fact that there are basically *no books* in it? Do you really want to be telling the whole world, 'Yes, my backpack is empty and *so is my damn head*'?"

Seb had insisted he hadn't been shoplifting—he'd just been walking around the store holding a set of headphones in the same hand as his sweatshirt and mindlessly walked out without paying for them.

No one could remember the last time something good had been attached to Seb Harris's name. His favorite uncle had been killed at the World Trade Center, which only served to give even more of an aura to an already compelling boy. He was popular, but you kept your distance, like you would from a tall tree in a lightning storm. People were just grateful he was there, or they themselves might be toast.

▼　●　▲

"So let's talk about cheating," said Ms. Vallis. "Was he or wasn't he?"

"He definitely was," insisted Deena. "I mean, it sure seems like it to *me*, anyway. When somebody drops a pencil on purpose during a test, isn't that always what they're trying to do? Look at their neighbor's answers?"

One week after Nick Thompson's visit, the talk in the eleven-thirty Writers' Workshop had turned to tricky questions about the Fruit Bowl story. No one but Corey had turned in their piece for the assignment yet, but they'd at least started *thinking* about writing them, which is how most writers spend half their time. And the thinking was getting interesting.

"It's totally subjective!" protested Ben. "We don't *know* if he was cheating. It just depends on what point of view you write from. The girl, Zoe, might think he was cheating when he really wasn't!"

"But let's say it's written from, like, the bird's-eye view, right?" said Fish, leaning into the argument. "The God's-eye view, so to speak, like it's a movie." Fish was always using expressions like "so to speak," and so was difficult to argue with. "That's the version that would be closest to the Immutable Truth of the fruit in the bowl, like Nick was talking about, meaning what *really happened*, right? Because in any story, when you're reading it, you're conscious that this is some writer's *version* of what happened, right? And a movie is less like that. It's the most real-seeming way of telling a story, by *showing* what really happened. Like life."

"But in a movie you just *see* what the actions are, just Kevin dropping the pencil and bumping Zoe and telling the joke and Jason laughing and everything," added Talisa Guzman. "In writing you can say things about people's thoughts and feelings and stuff."

"Excellent point," said Ms. Vallis. She turned to the board and wrote POINT OF VIEW.

"How many different accounts of what happened can we

get from different points of view?" she asked rhetorically. They all knew by this point in their education that the response was very likely "infinite" or at least "lots."

"I'm writing Zoe's point of view!" Jenna called out, waving her arm. "Definitely."

This set off a small skirmish among the girls. Talisa and Stephanie Jones had also wanted to write monologues that told Zoe's side of the story. Ms. Vallis, after a moment's thought, made the call that each of the main characters' points of view should be assigned to someone, so there wouldn't be too many of that genre, and that Jenna would write Zoe's side.

"Yeah!" crowed Jenna.

"You're such a brat, Jenna," Stephanie muttered.

"Talisa, remember you can write the story in a style that *sounds* like some Valley Girl–type description if you want," said Ms. Vallis. "Like, let's say, something that completely exaggerates every single detail of it?"

Talisa liked this idea a lot. "Yeaaaaah." She smiled, thinking.

Ms. Vallis scanned the room, her eyes calculating everything she knew about these students in one long sweep.

"Let's seeeee . . . Jason's side. Amir. Do you have an idea you're working on yet?"

He didn't. Jason's point of view went to Amir.

"Okaaaaay . . . now *Kevin's* side." Half the boys' hands went up. "Jeez, that's a lot of you who haven't started anything yet! How many people haven't even started it yet?"

Half the class's hands crept up. *"Get going!"* she mock-hollered. "Whaddoo I have to do to motivate you guys? I brought in a darn *rock star!*"

Embarrassed laughter.

"Okay, Kevin's point of view," she continued, "goes toooooooo . . ." She strolled the aisle thoughtfully through a sea-grass field of listlessly waving hands. "Seb."

Seb's hand, as usual, had not been raised. He looked up at Ms. Vallis with the slack face of someone who's just pulled into the wrong train station.

"What?"

"You're writing the story from Kevin's point of view."

"The dude who drops the pencil?"

"Yeah. Think you can do that?"

"Sure," he said with a shrug. " 'I dropped my pencil today.' I think I can handle that."

Titters.

"Great." Ms. Vallis smiled. "Maybe a *little* more effort than that."

"Then I guess Seb gets the final word about Kevin's guilt or innocence," Pearl cracked. "Right? His point of view is the only way to find out."

There was what can only be described as an awkward silence as Seb's shoplifting incident popped into everyone's heads.

"Hey! An Awkward Silence!" announced Seb, which broke it perfectly.

As the end of class neared, the issue of the Joke came up.

What was funny enough to make Jason laugh so hard milk comes out of his nose? It was a tough one. A few mediocre jokes were auditioned. Rosie knew a lot of the "guy walks into a bar" variety, but they were only funny when told in a relentless series. They needed one good one. Many tried and failed. Mia McCabe-Alvarez finally made the point that you can just *say* a joke was told without quoting the actual joke. "It can just be a very accurate report of *exactly what happened*," she said brusquely. "Without all the points of view and quotes and writery stuff. Right? I mean, isn't that a perfectly fine way to tell it?" Mia was a star athlete, an Amazon of a girl, keenly focused on anything and everything she set her mind to.

"Perfectly fine," said Ms. Vallis. "And interesting, too, Mia."

The lunch bell rang.

"That's good news," Greta announced as the class was dismissed. "Because I still think this story is too lame for words. Literally."

"Okay, I accept the challenge!" Fish boomed as he rose. "The very funny joke, as told to Jason, will appear in the screenplay version."

As the room emptied, Emily and Katie lingered by Ms. Vallis's desk.

"I'm writing the teacher's point of view, okay?" Emily said. "Is that a good one?"

"*Ohhhhhhhh*, Ms. McGee, you *do* know how to work it, don't you, sweetheart!" Ms. Vallis kidded, but she was pleased. "Go ahead. Great idea."

"Yay! I'll meet you out front, Katie," Emily trilled, and she danced out.

Katie was a fan of Ms. Vallis's in a way that felt like a secret crush. There are kids who do well because they want to please themselves, and kids who do well to please teachers. Then there are kids who do well because they want to be sure their teachers are not merely pleased with them but actually *admire* them. To know that the teacher will someday say to people, and to themselves, "I had Katie Parker in my class."

"I've started working on a fairy tale," Katie said, sliding her notebook into her plaid messenger bag. Ms. Vallis noticed there was a little matching wallet attached to a chain inside.

"I'm thrilled that's the genre you picked! You'll have a lot of fun with that, huh?"

"Yeah," said Katie, eyes down. "Because it's kind of like it's Zoe's point of view, but she's a fairy princess, in a fantasy way that shows even *more* fully who she is than another style would, you know?"

"Absolutely," enthused Ms. Vallis. "That's it in a nutshell! That's what makes literature so wonderful! The choices the writer makes. The choices that reveal the world to us."

"I think I wanna be a writer," Katie said, with a shyness previously nowhere to be found in her personality. "I really, really love it."

"That would be fantastic, Katie." Ms. Vallis smiled.

"If being a doctor doesn't work out. Or a model."

Ms. Vallis laughed very hard. They both did.

▼ ● ▲

Jenna and Stephanie usually twisted the combinations at their neighboring lockers in silence. They were never actually hostile to each other, but simply coexisted the way a monkey and a rabbit would coexist: lovelessly, and with absolutely nothing in common but fur. But Jenna felt a little guilty about her grab for the Zoe point of view in class and thought a small apology might be due.

"Sorry if I seemed a little pushy in class," she said to Stephanie's profile. "I just really wanted to do the Zoe monologue."

Stephanie shot her a dazzling smile, and for a second Jenna thought it was genuine. "And what Jenna really wants is important to *all* of us!" she said sarcastically, slamming her locker shut.

To Stephanie's annoyance, Jenna's eyes welled up with tears. Couldn't this girl simply let someone hate her?

"It just seemed to me that Zoe's type is, y'know, kinda *me* . . . and not really so much you or Talisa-ish . . . she's more like, fashion-ish and 'popular,'" Jenna said with what was meant to be a self-deprecating eye roll, "and cares too much about things—"

"Oh, and it takes *being* a Zoe to write about a Zoe?" Stephanie snapped. "Maybe I happen to understand a hell of a lot more than you know. See ya." She turned and walked briskly toward the computer room. Jenna dabbed her eyes quickly in a little mirror mounted inside her locker door.

Katie bounced to her side. "You coming to lunch?"

"Yeah," Jenna said. "Did you know Stephanie could be a total be-*atch*?"

They passed Stephanie talking to a teacher outside the computer room. Katie was absorbed in a steady stream of chatter, so she missed the moment when Jenna and Stephanie looked straight into each other's eyes for the very first time. Jenna had to look away.

▼ ● ▲

The computer room was always fairly busy, before, during, and after school. But at lunchtime it was taken over by the few kids who were desperately in need of it, usually for overdue projects. Stephanie was a regular, not because she was a negligent student, but because the computer her family had at home was such a clanking antique it was useless, and they had no Internet access.

Belinda was a lunchtime newcomer. She was hunched over a keyboard when Stephanie entered, and she looked up only to smile sheepishly.

"Is this the one you usually use?" she asked. "Because I don't care, I can move."

"That's okay, I'm good here," Stephanie said as she settled nearby. Justin Sirk sat with his back to them at another computer, eavesdropping, tinkering with the school Web site. He was such a wirehead he found nonvirtual relationships challenging. Thai Wheeler sat at a keyboard two down from Belinda, hammering away at missed homework.

"All our computers at home are down," Belinda groaned to

Stephanie. "My dad put in a wireless hub, but it's not working right."

"What a drag," Stephanie commiserated. "Ours is down too."

"I have this amazing idea for the Fruit Bowl project, and I really wanna get the info I need for it before I forget it."

"Yeah? What's the idea?"

"It's kind of strange—you're probably gonna think I'm really weird." Belinda bit her lip-glossed lip. "I got this idea to tell the story with *only math*. Like, just the measurements of everything."

Thai looked up at this. Even Justin turned around.

"Woo!" said Thai appreciatively. "Very cool!" Thai was everyone's ideal boyfriend, a faintly clove-scented poet with a rock band. He was also coolly modest and hadn't even mentioned the band to Nick Thompson.

"I need to find out what the decibel level of a loud cafeteria might be. . . ." She trailed off, squinting at the computer. "Anyway . . . whatever. Sorry. I'll be quiet now."

Stephanie, Thai, and Justin looked at her, their sweet, ditzy Belinda, then at each other over her head, and cracked up with the sheer surprise of it.

"What?" Belinda looked up innocently, then joined them. *"What?"* She giggled, smacking Thai.

▼ ● ▲

New York Bites (yes, that's really the name) was the sit-down deli of choice for Max Baum-White, Jonathan Fleck-Fishman, Yun Li, and Gary Beemer. If hyphens were found to have anything to do with IQ, the four very successful parents of Max and Jonathan would not be one bit surprised.

"Stop displacing that liquid with gas!" Max mock-scolded, laughing hysterically as Yun blew into a Snapple with a straw.

"Yeah, desist from displacing that damn liquid with expelled carbon dioxide!" shrieked Jonathan, doubled over with howls.

"Yo, ixnay on the ubbles-bay, ude-day!" screamed Gary.

"Oh my God! Yun's name in Pig Latin is tough!" said Max.

"Un-yay Ee-lay," Yun pronounced. "Yeah, wow, tough! Get a life, American morons."

Danielle and Mia strolled in for sandwiches to go.

"Hi, Danielle!" called Jonathan.

"Hi," she tossed back.

"You guys both gonna visit Bronx Science?" Yun called.

A lot of the smart kids would be applying to the very selective math and science high schools this fall.

"Maybeeee," Mia sang.

The boys fell silent, momentarily forgetting what they'd been talking about.

Danielle and Mia left a swirl of shampoo and citrus behind as they passed the boys and headed out the door.

"Bye!" Gary yelled to the empty air.

"Nice talkin' to ya!" Max shouted.

"Ice-nay oobs-bay!" Jonathan hollered.

Hysteria.

"Thanks!" Danielle yelled playfully, sticking her head back in the doorway, then out again.

Conniptions.

▼ ● ▲

Chardinay King lowered herself carefully onto the playground bench. Her knee was hurting again, but she was afraid to tell her mother, because she was afraid her mom would take her to the doctor, who would once again tell her how urgently she needed to lose weight.

She delicately spread out a paper napkin on the bench beside her, reached into a paper bag from the A&P deli counter, and laid out her lunch with the sublime dignity of a tea ceremony.

Tuna salad sandwich. Diet Pepsi. Macaroni salad. Doritos. Shrink-wrapped slice of marble cake. Snack-size Nestlé's Buncha Crunch.

She ate it all, very slowly, with her manicured pinky raised, the way her family always teased her about. She was a happy girl. She rubbed her knee as she ate, and watched the grade-school kids playing on the swings, and in her mind she was swinging too, like she used to, with her legs like arrows and her head thrown back to the sky.

▼ ● ▲

"Sorry!" Rob panted as his basketball hit the chain link fence behind Chardinay, startling her. "His fault!" He pointed at Jawshua, who feinted and smashed it out of Rob's hands again. They ricocheted down the sidewalk, Rob, Jawshua, Corey, Amir, and Seb, like some sharp-kneed, many-limbed cartoon of tangled bodies.

Rob was wearing, inexplicably, a pink plastic bag on his head.

"Love the hat, Rob!" Carly trilled.

"Thanks, wanna borrow it?"

Amir body-slammed him into the fence.

Rob slid down like loose mercury, unhurt, and flew toward school at the head of the pack.

"I wanna be Rob in my next life," said Carly wistfully. "Don't you?"

"Ahhhh, no thanks," said Emily.

"He doesn't care what anybody thinks. Ever. He's just . . . happy. With a stupid pink bag on his head. How is that possible?"

"Sports," sneered Cassie. "He's obsessed with sports, and only sports. Nothing *but* sports. Basketball, football, baseball, soccer, hockey—"

"We *get* it, Cassie, we *get* it," cried Katie. "Sports!"

"Sorry," Cassie said, blushing. "I know I talk too much."

"Do you? We hadn't noticed," Jocelyn teased, and flung her arm around her as they all streamed back into school.

▼　●　▲

Here are the notable things that happened in the three days leading up to Nick Thompson's return:

Fish Koenig came up with the perfect joke for his screenplay and couldn't resist telling everyone.
Cameron Haas asked Emily McGee to the movies but

she said no; then he saw her there later with Ben
Rizzo.

Graham Beckwith announced he was leaving West
Side Middle and transferring to an East Side pri-
vate school October fifth.

Morgan Greenwald broke her thumb when she was hit
by a bike messenger.

Seb Harris went missing.

It was Tuesday morning and his mother called the school
office to get him the message that he'd left his notebook at
home, which he'd be needing for an open-notebook history
test that day. She was put on hold while someone went to find
him to see if she should bring it. She was not at all pleased to
be informed that he wasn't even in school, he'd been marked
absent. The school promised they'd call her the minute he
walked in.

He didn't. The school day passed with no sign of Seb.

His mother's mood followed the usual parental arc from
anger to worry to frantic fear as the day progressed. She called
every one of his friends after school, who fully realized that a
cover-up wasn't in order, the truth was. But no one had a
shred of information.

The late September days were getting shorter. At a little
after five-thirty, the streets looked dusky, the entire city
seemed blanketed with vague threats. She was about to call
the police to officially report him missing, her neighbor's
arm around her, Seb's notebook and his CDs and his dirty

clothes and anything he'd ever touched a pulsing, heart-breaking vignette of potential grief.

Then the phone rang. She lunged for it like a jungle animal. "Hello?"

"Hi," said Seb.

A flood of tears. She couldn't speak; her relief and her anger were competing too fiercely.

"Where are you? *Where are you?*" she finally managed.

"At a diner downtown," he said. Then his own voice was ragged with tears. "Near the World Trade Center."

They were like a kind of weeping bellows then, the mother and the son, sounding like one was wetly keening outward as the other drew breath, then inhaling as the other cried out. Then their words finally returned.

"He's not there, Mom. It's just a construction site."

"I know, sweetie," she snuffled. "I know."

"He's *so* not there. There are only tourists there. And that Century 21 discount store. Which you would no doubt *die* over. If Uncle Dan hadn't. Y'know . . . died."

There was a beat while her heart decided which way to go. Then they broke into the giddy laughter of the spent, the frayed, the beloved.

"Get your butt home," she said. "Wherever he is, he's happy you at least figured out where he's not." Then, "I love you so, so much."

▼   ●   ▲

The word of Seb's being "found" got around fast that night, and Ms. Vallis was as relieved as everyone else. But she begged off the phone quickly to get back to the task at hand, straight through dinner (scrambled eggs) and two movies (*All About Eve, Waiting for Guffman*).

Forty-nine pieces from forty-eight kids. (Gary Beemer had submitted two.) Plus a bonus from "Anonymous." Her fingers were nearly bleeding from pushing brass fasteners through fifty books, including one with a dedication page for Nick: *To the nerd with the reading glasses and the notebook. Love, the West Side Middle School 8th Grade.*"

She squinted at the clock as she slapped the last book onto the stack: 1:27 a.m. And then she couldn't resist reading one of them cover to cover, sitting up in her bed with a bag of Goldfish, after which she did what most good teachers do . . . cried, and laughed at herself for it, whether from exhaustion or pride, who cares which, they're both signs of a job well done.

▼ ● ▲

"I didn't care if they found him or not, dawg," said David, "as long as he turned in his *story*! He did, right?"

"Yeah," Ms. Vallis laughed.

"So was Kevin cheating or not?" Diz prodded.

"You'll seeee," she teased.

The entire eighth grade, plus teachers who canceled classes, plus Nick Thompson, was gathered in what was called the Large Studio. They wouldn't have been able to fit into any classroom, and the lack of desks in the studio let everyone arrange themselves naturally, the way crystals do. Nick was somewhat central, of course, being the guest of honor. He was wearing blue jeans and a white shirt and sneakers today, and his promised reading glasses. Ms. Vallis gave him a lot of credit for understanding that this time it wasn't about him.

The books were piled on a table enticingly, the way trophies are at a banquet. Everyone was kind of jabbering, more slap-happy than usual, sitting sloped against each other on the floor, on low bookshelves, on benches. Max, Yun, Gary, and Danielle were taking turns showing off to each other, noodling gently on the piano. Thai was playing with Belinda's hair. Pearl, Tionna, Rosie, and Stephanie were swaying back and forth, singing made-up words to "Kumbaya" and giggling. Rob, Justin, Maeve, and Katie kept trying to peek inside the books.

Fish was giving a running commentary to Nick.

"Observe," he said, "the very touching, familial, you might even say *circus-freak* closeness of the eighth grade." Then he did a comical, sentimental mock sob.

But he was only half kidding.

Because the Fruit Bowl Project had changed things a little. There was a sense of happy expectation in even the rumor of each other's efforts, a pride in the sheer variety of each other's gifts and weirdnesses they'd never felt before. In books an inch thick, piled in two-foot stacks, were their talents made visible.

They felt, collectively, awesome.

"We're still waiting for Seb, A.J., and Cassie," said Ms. Vallis.

Cassie ran in breathlessly and took a seat next to Talisa. "Sorry! Subway."

"Ohmigod," laughed Talisa. "That's the shortest excuse I've ever heard you give!"

Seb sauntered in with a plastic grocery bag, A.J. shuffling behind.

"Awriiiight, let's get started!" Nick enthused.

"Woo, woo, woo, woo! Seb, Seb, Seb, Seb!" A little chant began, riding a goofy wave. "Did he *cheat*? Did he *cheat*?"

"Shhh!" Ms. Vallis admonished. "Chill."

"Got a present for you," Seb announced.

He walked over to where Ms. Vallis sat and reached into the plastic bag. He placed a shiny red apple on the table in front of her.

"Woooo!" They all stomped and laughed appreciatively. "Apple for the teachahhhhh!"

"Very nice." She smiled wryly at Seb. "Thank you very much, Seb."

There was more in the bag. Mugging to his audience, he pulled out a bunch of bananas and put them on the table.

"Oooooh!" The room applauded.

A pear. Two oranges. A kiwi. A bunch of grapes. "Ahhhhh!"

Ms. Vallis's face was three shades of happiness.

The pile of fruit sat there like an off-kilter centerpiece, and Seb took a seat.

Ms. Vallis made a little speech of thanks to Nick. The

entire class gave him a standing ovation, and Emily gave him flowers, and Jawshua presented him with the first book.

"I can't read," he confessed with a moan in a Brit accent. "Forgot to tell you that part. Rock star, don'tcha know. Never needed to."

(Belinda believed him for a second.)

Then:

"Let's pass these suckers out!"

Kids were enlisted to hand out all the books. The plan was to have any author who wanted, read their piece out loud. Which they all did, to the sound of cheers, amazement, laughter, and high-fiving.

But mostly to the sweet sound of their not-so-tough audience's rapt, undivided attention.

Here's what they wrote. Ms. Vallis had sweated out the order a bit, littering the floor of her apartment with index cards like fallen leaves. But in the end, it was precisely the lesson of leaves that struck her as right. She'd shuffled them around intuitively—bright red, tattered, gold—without thinking much, then stood back from the canvas and thought . . . *Perfect*. Much like the eighth grade itself.

THE
FRUIT BOWL
PROJECT

by

The West Side Middle School Eighth Grade

Contents

JUST THE FACTS
By Greta Stern

One morning in a sixth-grade classroom in New York City, a boy dropped a pencil during a test. Stooping to pick it up, he bumped the arm of a girl sitting next to him. She got mad at him, the bump having caused her to make a mark on her test, and accused him of trying to cheat. Later, in the cafeteria, the same boy told a joke to another boy, who then laughed, making his drink come out of his nose. They had to throw their lunches away.

PRECISELY
By Mia McCabe-Alvarez

It was April 20 at 11:05 a.m. in room 502 of I.S. 280 in New York City, New York. Twenty-eight sixth-grade students were approximately midway through the ELA Reading Test administered by the City of New York when twelve-year-old Kevin Marchetti, a 5' 6", 133-lb. dark-haired male, dropped a pencil. Whether this act was accidental or purposeful is unclear. However, we know that in the course of retrieving the pencil from the floor, Mr. Marchetti bumped the female immediately adjacent to him, the 4'10½", 94-lb. brown-haired Zoe Blass, eleven, in the right elbow. This action caused Ms. Blass's pencil to move across her paper in such a way as to make an errant one-inch mark in the shape of a crescent. Ms. Blass perceived Mr. Marchetti's actions to be deliberate and aggressive, and possibly an attempt to observe Ms. Blass's test answers. She was consequently angered enough to direct a tirade of verbal abuse at Mr. Marchetti. Mr. Marchetti issued no apology or comment, but continued to attend to the task of completing the test. Ms. Blass also returned to said task, after making an only partially successful attempt to erase the pencil mark.

A short time later, at 12:17 p.m. in the basement cafeteria of the school, Mr. Marchetti was relating a joke to classmate Jason Allen, a 4'11", 82-lb. red-haired male. In his amusement, Mr. Allen inadvertently aspirated Hershey's Chocolate Milk into his sinuses and expelled it forcefully out of his nose and onto Mr. Marchetti's lunch of chicken nuggets and Santa Fe potato skins. Mr. Marchetti and Mr. Allen then disposed of Mr. Marchetti's lunch in the cafeteria's central trash receptacle. There are dramatically differing reports of both disgust and high excitement among the students gathered, Ms. Blass among them.

ZOE'S SIDE
By Jenna Bromberg

God, I cannot believe how hot it was
during that test, I was, like, *sweating.*
I probably should've worn my striped halter
but after that whole stupid thing last
year about a dress code I'm practically
afraid to.

So let me tell you what happened. I was
innocently working on the test when Kevin
drops his pencil, completely on purpose.
He's always looking for any excuse to bug
me or talk to me, ALWAYS. The pathetic
thing is that he actually thinks I have a
crush on him, and nothing I say or do seems
to prove to him that I don't. I used to
have a small one, but he's been really
gross and stupid for the last two years.
Anyway, he's picking up his pencil and all
of a sudden he goes like BAM! right into my
writing arm! And my arm goes, like,
flying across the paper and makes a huge
mark on my test!

I have a very bad temper, I can't help
it, my mom calls me Miss Diva from Hell.
Plus I cry very easily—when I'm either mad,
sad, or happy, I just cry. So I flipped out

a little, I admit it. I was just so upset that somebody would do something so stupid, and the test is really important. I have a lot of pressure on me, to be smart, not just pretty, like my sister, Ariel. It's a LOT of pressure. And I suddenly just hated Kevin so much I exploded, because he doesn't understand that kind of pressure at all, he just laughs at anyone who cares about anything. I told Ms. Petricoff he was cheating, and I feel kind of bad about that because I don't even think it was true. But if I apologize for that part he'll just add it into the evidence he thinks he has that I like him, so I'm definitely never apologizing. Besides, Ms. Petricoff hardly even got mad at him, as usual. I swear the only way to get positive attention at this school is to be a loser. It really seems that way sometimes. And that kind of hurts, because I'm just not a loser.

He told some joke at lunch that made Jason Allen laugh so hard his drink came out his nose all over his chicken nuggets. Talk about losers.

LYRIC
By Cameron Haas

[VERSE:]
Oh, oh . . .
My head is spinnin' . . .
This stupid test must be
Gettin' the best of me
Oh, no . . .
He dropped a pencil . . .
He's leanin' close to you
Doesn't he know what I'm goin' through?

Oh girl
Don't make a bigger mistake
Oh girl
How long is it gonna take
Till you
See that he'll never be right?
Cuz I'm the one who loves you,
Standin' here in plain sight!

[CHORUS:]
I may be laughin' on the outside
But baby, on the inside
Is overflowin' love
4 U . . .
I wanna promise you the whole world

Even that chocolate milk, girl,
is sprayin' out my nose
4 U . . .

[BRIDGE:]
Oh baby, 4 U . . .
4 U . . .
It's true . . .
Everything that I do is 4 U . . .

RAP
By David Edelman (aka Lil' Dee)

Verse 1: Another morning and I'm slavin' at the desk / ball-an'-chained to the test, it's messed up / C'mon, I'm goin' mental! / Gotta be droppin' my pencil! / It's one step for mankind, a bland kinda Zoe jolt / Call it my little revolt, cuz I'm revoltin' / I'm entertainin' you folks / I only meant to bend on over, pick it up / Yo, I only hit her arm / the crazy girl made such a drama! / (chorus) Sorry, Zoe / I never meant to hit you / I never meant to make you cry / Hey, I'm just pickin up my pencil / I'm sorry, Zoe / I never meant to hit you / I know ya think I cheated, yo / But I'm just pickin up my pencil.
Verse 2: The cafeteria, sixth-grade hysteria / Can't hardly hear ya but I'm makin it clear to ya I'm the joker / and so I'm tellin a joke / Yeah, c'mon, welcome to my slippery slope / Cuz I'm the Kevin Marchetti, yeah I'm the king / I

know ya may think I'm irritat-ing / But here the crowd is, they know what funny is, loud is / No thanks to Mama that I'm feelin' what proud is / Jason, they know the face but can't place him / Yeah, Zoe and her crazy chickens just erase him.

Verse 3: Not me, yeah, not the Kevin Marchetti / I'm comin at ya like a plate a' spaghetti / I'm like the penny always turns up bad, and always burns up mad, and ain'tcha glad, ain'tcha glad you ain't gotta do it? / You're happy I'ma go through it? / You gotta let me cuz I'm the Marchetti / And lucky you, you're never gonna forget me / Yeah I'm the man who got the rhymes and the prose, so good you know how it goes, ya blow milk outa your nose! / Yeah, I'm the man who got the rhymes and the prose, so good you know how it goes, ya blow milk outa your nose!

LIMERICK
By Corey Lewis

With thumbs that were barely prehensile
An oafish young lad flipped a pencil
When his nuggets got shot
With some chocolate milk snot
He cracked up like all sixth-grade gents'll.

FAIRY TALE
By Katie Parker

Once upon a time, in a city not far, there was a school, quite like the school you may know. It was made of bricks, and wood, and iron, and, yes, of chalk, and dares, and sticky things under the chairs. But it was . . . well, I shall just come right out and say it, or I shan't hold your interest for very long, shall I?

It was just a little bit magic.

In this school there was a young maiden named Zoe with hair as brown as polished mahogany, skin as fair as new cream, and eyes the color of an ocean not yet named. She seemed much like any ordinary pretty girl, except that she was not ordinary, not at all. She was, unknown to all, an enchanted princess.

Princess Zoe sat in her classroom on a hot morning in the month of April, watching dreamily as tiny stars of golden dust danced in a ray of sunlight.

Is today the day? she wondered with a sigh. *Shall the spell be broken today?*

For eleven long years the princess had waited patiently in the pleasant slumber of a commoner's life. All knew her simply as Zoe, a quick-witted girl held in high regard by the other children, much loved by her hardworking guardians. But like a sunflower stretching ever closer to the light, Zoe was a princess awaiting the love of her prince. Only then could she claim her throne and return to the enchanted land that was her birthright. And as her true mother the queen had foretold at her birth, his name was . . .

She knew not! These are the words the queen had spoken, as much a riddle to Zoe now as they had been in all the years she'd heard them repeated by her loving guardians:

> *Tenth of the letters he shall be*
> *Not the next, who tortures thee!*
> *Short of stature, cap of rose*
> *Spilling laughter from his nose!*

Pray, Queen, what didst thou mean? Princess Zoe nearly cried aloud, so keen was her hope on this bright morning. But no, she had not spoken aloud, and no answer came from the common, ragged children who surrounded her. She bent to her task, her lily-soft hand working the pencil as best she could, and a teardrop fell like dew, unseen.

Goodness as pure and deep as that of Princess Zoe must always, it seems, be tested. And sure enough, in the heart of a dark boy named Kevin dwelt her soul's opposite. Kevin was a cruel jester by nature, always attempting to attract the fair princess's eye. Today, he dropped his pencil to the floor beneath her writing desk with a mischievous flourish.

"A pox on me!" exclaimed Kevin, mocking her delicacy, his contrition as hollow as a gourd. "I fear I have dropped my pencil!"

Princess Zoe's cheeks flushed pink, and she would not meet his trollish gaze. Kevin bent double to retrieve the pencil, then clumsily rose from the floor. So clumsily, in fact, that his shoulder struck the princess's arm as she wrote! She looked down at her paper, her fine and lovely script besmirched by a jagged scrawl, and anger ruled her heart.

"What dost thou think thou art doing?" she cried. "Behold the ugliness thou hast wrought! And purloining my *answers*, forsooth!"

The other children gazed at her in wonderment. Always they had considered Zoe a rare and special flower among them, but alas, she could also be one unstable maiden. Kevin's mocking visage remained unrepentant. And the door to the princess's heart, once more, was slammed and shuttered as she endured her plight.

The sun made its arc to the after-noon, and with a heavy heart the princess ate a small repast with her most favoured young maids. Her spirit ached with the knowledge that yet another day had nearly passed, and still the mystery of her prince and saviour's identity had not been solved. Would she never return home?

At a nearby table, a young redheaded lad named Jason ate with the roguish Kevin. They laughed as they ate, at what boorish nonsense the princess cared not. The queen's riddle drifted idly into her thoughts, as it had so often done before:

> *Tenth of the letters he shall be*
> *Not the next, who tortures thee!*
> *Short of stature, cap of rose . . .*

As if by a bolt of lightning, the princess suddenly saw the boys Kevin and Jason anew. The tenth letter of the alphabet!

The letter *J*. Could it be, could it truly be . . . Jason? Short of stature, cap of rose! Yes, it could indeed be he! And the next, the letter *K*, surely it was Kevin who was her torturer!

Zoe beheld the unlikely messenger of her deliverance. Sweet Jason, dear Jason, who had always cherished her from afar. The princess's joy knew no bounds. Hope breathed life into her dormant heart. But how could she be certain? What, pray tell, was the meaning of the last line of the poem? Only then would she know the truth.

And then, as she watched, what happened next made the very heavens sing. Lifting a vessel to his lips, Jason laughed heartily, and his draught projected mightily from his nose.

Spilling laughter from his nose!

Finally, the princess dared to believe. *It is he,* her heart rejoiced. *My prince is Jason!*

Then, just as certainly, *Ew.*

And the princess vowed, forevermore, to keep it to herself.

Haiku
By Maeve Gillis

A pencil is dropped
Small sword in a small battle
Ending in nose milk

NEWSPAPER
By Deena Prajapati

NEW YORK—When is an accident not an accident?

When it's "totally on purpose," said Zoe Blass, eleven, of Manhattan. The sixth grader at I.S. 280 said it began innocently enough. The kids were taking a citywide reading test the morning of April 20 and Blass was, she insists, doing very well.

"I always do well on those tests," she said. "I always think I might flunk, but then I always do well. It's weird."

Weirder still was what happened next, reported Blass. A classmate, Kevin Marchetti, dropped his pencil on the floor and bent to pick it up.

"He, like, slammed into me," said Blass emphatically. "I mean, not just a little bump. He hit my elbow really, really hard." Blass also claims Marchetti was attempting to cheat, though she's unable to prove it. The incident left her close to tears and with an ugly pencil mark on her test. Blass claimed Marchetti gave no apology.

Other students backed up Blass's account. "He, like, slammed her," agreed

65

Franny Stabenau. "He totally did," chimed in Lindsey Edwards.

But there is, the girls reported, some justice. Later on in the cafeteria, another student, Jason Allen, laughed so hard at a joke Marchetti told, chocolate milk sprayed out of his nose and all over his and Marchetti's lunch.

"It was gross," Blass said. "But he deserved it."

"Totally," agreed Stabenau.

TRAGEDY
By Carly Heywood

The children sat trapped in the stifling room, slender
backs hunched at their cramped desks, fists wrapped tight
around pencils worn as dull as their anguished minds.
Guilty of nothing but the crime of being eleven years old,
they were sentenced to this, yet another cruel test, while
outside the April morning taunted them.

But one boy, one special boy, had thoughts other than
broken obedience on this morning. In one last, desperate
expression of his thwarted, aching spirit, he sent his
pencil tumbling to the floor. Would anyone notice? he
wondered. Would someone, anyone, see this message in a
bottle thrown from his soul into the abyss?

But it was not to be. No one saw. No one cared. They
were all well past caring. And now . . . so was he.

He bent down, so low it appeared a prisoner's prayer,
and fumbled for the sad, chewed pencil on the grimy
floor below. Then, finding it, he rose.

And rose.

And unstoppably . . . irrevocably . . . rose.

Was it fate that stepped in then, and made it all,
without warning, go so terribly wrong? The girl didn't see
it coming, surely. And just as certainly, the boy had no
violent intent. But it all, everything, forever, changed.

Boy. Rising.
Shoulder. Approaching.
Girl. Writing.
Elbow. Jutting.
And then, sickeningly . . . the crash.

At impact, the young girl's pencil careened across the page in a crazy arc. It almost seemed to happen in slow motion as she struggled to regain control, struggled and lost, the pencil carving a path of destruction fully an inch long. Perhaps she screamed, perhaps, as in a nightmare, no sound emerged from her gaping mouth. The last thing she remembered seeing was the boy's unrepentant, unfeeling face.

And then the silence. The agonized silence, and the erasing that can never, ever be.

Time heals. Children forget. Bells ring, and there is forever, mercifully, lunch. And laughter.

And chocolate milk, always, projecting from a young boy's nose.

But one girl watches, and she will forget nothing. And she will think, forever:

Why?
Why?
Why?

CHATTY
By Cassie DiGiovanni

The funniest thing happened this morning at school! There were a lot of people—well, not really <u>people</u>, I mean kids, not that kids aren't people, but you know, younger. And they were in one of the rooms of the school, one of the classrooms, right? And it was really really hot, I don't mean like ouch hot, like a stove, or you know, sticking your finger in a candle, which my sister actually does, but like weather hot. And the kids were taking a test. Like reading, and then writing answers, and then giving it to the teacher when you're done. Anyway, one of the kids drops his pencil, and he leans out of his chair—he's sitting in a chair, maybe I didn't mention that. He's in a chair. They all are. Were. Anyway, he leans, not like way out, but partway. If he leaned all the way he could fall out, which has happened to me before, believe it or not—I fell out of a chair once. But it wasn't to pick up something I dropped, it was to look at a bug, in my case. But anyway, he leaned down to get the pencil, and when he was getting up he hit a girl! Not like hit her with his fist, like "hit," I guess that's kind of confusing, I shouldn't say "hit," but he like bumped her, he bumped the part of your arm that bends. Not yours, the girl's. The part of her arm that bends was sticking out, the elbow, because she was writing. And her pencil makes like a mark, a line that's a mistake, that she didn't mean to make. And the girl was really angry, really mad, I mean you could see it in her face. Not you but the people who were there could, the people who happened to be looking, that is, could see it in her face that she was mad. Plus she was yelling about it, so even if you were blind, or just not looking, you could tell she was mad, and she said he was probably trying to cheat! As in look at her paper. And she thought the boy should apologize for hitting her, or say "I'm sorry," or "excuse me," or "oops," or whatever people say when they hit someone, unless you're like a professional boxer, that kind of hitting. Although as I said, this was not that kind of hitting. Anyway, he didn't say anything! He was just silent. Well, I mean, except for his breathing, which he of course had to do or he'd die. Or he'd faint at least—you faint first so that you actually <u>won't</u> die, your body just breathes without you having to think about it when you faint. Anyway, so he wasn't literally totally silent, he was breathing. And probably his pencil made some kind of little scritchy sound on the paper when he went back to writing. Which he did—he went back to writing. And the girl did too. The one who he hit. Bumped. Which made her make the mark. Anyway, later on at lunch, still inside the same building, it's not like they, you know, went to a restaurant or something, they had lunch in the school, in the bottom of the building, the basement. There, I knew I'd think of it, the basement. God, I'm sorry, this is taking a really long time to tell, huh? Sorry, sorryyy, I'm almost finished. Wait. The boy who hit—ohmigod I mean <u>bumped</u>—God, am I lame!—the boy who bumped the girl was telling a story, a funny story, one of those short funny stories that you have to memorize? With an ending, a punch line? The kind I'm really bad at? As you can probably imagine? Knowing me? Well, not that you know me, at least not well anyway, but—wait, wait, I'm almost done! Anyway, he was telling a funny story to another boy, with red hair, not that that's important, but it happened to be red. It was <u>reddish</u>, not like "woo, I'm a clown" red, just somewhat reddish. Orangey undertones. Or overtones. Or whatever you call them. Anyway, this is the good part. The boy with the reddish hair was drinking chocolate milk, and he was laughing really hard, and the chocolate milk got all over the other boy's lunch! Oh wait, wait, ohmigod, I forgot to say the best part! Wait, I didn't say the best part! Ohmigod! Ha, ha! I told you I'm bad at stories! Anyway, how the chocolate milk got all over the boy's lunch is that it came out of the other boy's, the red-haired boy's, NOSE! And it sprayed all over the lunch. The chicken nuggets, or the Santa Fe potato skins, or maybe even both of them! And they couldn't stop laughing! Not literally, but they were laughing so, so, so, sooo hard. Because it was really gross, but in that way that's funny, that grossed-out but funny way? And they had to actually throw their lunches away! They went to the trash thing, the can, the more like barrel, and they dumped their whole lunch into it. Not like the tray, but all the food, and plates and sporks. And napkins. Actually I'm not sure about the napkins. They might not have even used napkins. Anyway they ran and

71

threw it away right after it happened, not like later, when the lunch period is over, when everybody usually throws their lunch away. Unless it's turkey wraps, which people usually like. People in school, I mean, when there's turkey wraps. Then again, some people bring their lunch, not knowing that it'll be turkey wraps that day, and then they trade it with someone who doesn't like turkey wraps. Although that's rare, because as I said, most people like them. Turkey wraps, I mean. And—wait! I'm almost done! Wait! . . .

TWENTY WORDS OR LESS
by Brendan Torres

School. Hot. Test. Boy. Restless. Pencil. Drop. Retrieve. Bump. Girl. Angry. Lunch. Boys. Joke. Laughter. Milk. Nose. Food. Gross. Trash.

JASON'S SIDE
By Amir Azzam

I worked really hard on the reading test this morning. I work hard on everything. Even if it's an easy question, I go over it twice, because I'm always nervous that if I think it's easy it can't be right. It was incredibly hot. My mind started to wander and I noticed Zoe's purple shoes. They were ridiculously thick, like overgrown cartoon flip-flops. I notice things that Zoe wears every day. She has a weird obvious crush on Kevin, but I'm the one who always notices what she wears.

All of a sudden he bumps into her and she freaks out, like "You made me make a mark on my test! Look what you made me do!" and she accuses him of cheating. I actually don't believe Kevin was cheating. I've known him since, like, first grade. He likes to stir things up but he's too smart to do something stupid like cheat. But he's been a little weird this year. Ms. Petricoff let him off pretty easy.

At lunch Kevin told me a great joke. I laughed so hard chocolate milk came out my nose all over our lunch. Seriously, all over the chicken nuggets, we had to throw them away. It was sick. It was so funny. It was the one time I was hoping Zoe wasn't watching, but she was. She looked at Kevin like he was God, and then she looked at me like I was . . . Jason.

ALIEN VISITATION
By Jawshua Perry

Field researcher easily gained access to stone
shelter labeled "I.S. 280" by temporarily brain-
vaporizing a young female Earthling and donning
vacated flesh and garments.

Researcher observed a pronounced tribal
interdependence among the young of this carbon-
based, moderately evolved species. They wielded
thin cylindrical instruments that produced
meaningful glyphs on white, rectangular sheets
of wood-derived tablature.

Much of interior environment is wood-derived,
both the individual platforms upon which the
creatures fold themselves into a position of rest
and those upon which they work, evidencing this
species's thorough utilization of the planet's
abundant oxygen-producing plant life. A notable
lack of oxygen was detected in this interior space,
however, which was perhaps a factor in one male's
sudden loss of motor control as a cylinder slipped
from his pincer-like grasp. Male was observed
retrieving cylinder and colliding with female in a
sudden and uncoordinated burst of movement.
Female displayed defensive, then violently
combative, posturing. Male's features remained

impassive. Male in question appears to be the least intelligent of grouping, yet physically dominant. This phenomenon has been noted species-wide.

Later observed creatures in boisterous group feeding ritual. Field researcher hid in cubicle labeled "Girls' Room" for much of ritual due to nearly unbearable sonic intensity. Limited observation revealed creatures to be voracious oral consumers of organic and pseudo-organic compounds possessing the predominant salient feature of "crispiness." Plant life in diet is curiously absent.

Dominant male was observed communicating information to subordinate male possessing atypical head-fur coloration. Subordinate male was then observed emitting strange whooping vocalizations similar to mammalian sea life. This appeared to be a display of pleasure. Subordinate male then exhibited unusual expulsion of brownish liquid from nasal blowholes. This prompted even more intense whooping vocalizations from both males, and in all group members in the immediate vicinity. The two males then deemed the edible organic compounds repellant and disposed of them in a large metallic cylinder.

TANKA
By Max Baum-White

Like cherry boughs bent
to their task are the children.
Dropped pencil, large boy
to a maid shows no sorrow.
Later, chicken nugget mirth.

EXAGGERATION
By Talisa Guzman

It was *easily* 100 degrees in there,
the room felt like a *pottery kiln* for
God's sake. The poor sixth graders were
practically *fainting*. As usual, the
teacher was hovering like some predatory
hawk while the kids were taking yet
another test in an *endless* series of
completely pointless tests. One huge boy
threw his pencil on the floor in absolute
disgust. He hit the sweet little girl next
to him when he picked it up and she cried
out in *agony*, the kids all stopped dead
they were so worried about her! It was
totally obvious to everyone that he was
probably *cheating,* and the teacher did
exactly *nothing* about it. The incredible
thing is he practically *laughed,* the
stupid thug! He's lucky he didn't get
expelled. She was a *crumpled heap* of sobs.
It was *so* awful.

Later in the cafeteria something
hysterical happened! The same exact
horrible boy told the funniest joke you've
ever heard in your entire *life*! The boy he
told it to laughed so hard chocolate milk

gushed out of his nose like an open *fire hydrant*, I mean *torrents* of chocolate milk, all over *everybody's* lunch trays! It was the most disgusting mess you've ever *seen*! People were lining up at the trash cans having a total *fit,* screaming and laughing and dumping *tons* of revolting food into the trash! It was complete, total *pandemonium*!!!

MEASUREMENTS
By Belinda Voskidis

23' x 18' classroom, 10'2" ceiling.

4 windows on south wall, each 46"W x 70"H.

28 students sit at 28 desks, each desk 26"W x 18"D x 30"H.

Air temp. 93 degrees.

7" pencil drops at 15 mph, hits floor at 56-degree angle, rolls 2'8" north, comes to stop 3/4" from and approx. parallel to 4" platform shoe.

Boy retrieves pencil, hits arm of adjacent girl approx 3" above elbow. Resulting pencil mark on girl's paper is 7/8" long.

Girl's yelling peaks at 92 dB, duration 31 seconds.

45' x 37' cafeteria, 9' ceiling.

6 windows on south wall, each 46"W x 70"H.

116 students eat at 8 tables measuring 10' x 4'.

Air temp. 82 degrees.

Crowd noise level peaks at 117 dB.

Punch line followed by 2.5-second reaction time and liquid expelled from nasal passages at 68 mph.

VICTORIAN
By Tionna Chapman

The youthful effort warmed the room
Yet more than April's sun.
The pencil drop't, the girlish frown,
And sturdy lad were one.
The heat that buzzed the classroom blinds
Did blind thee to the joy
Of test, and youth, and frown, and girl,
And life, and sweaty boy!

The lunchroom laughter made us vow
companions much less dumb,
The rubb'ry chicken smelled of hope
for better meals to come.
But would it were a sultry morn
When boys were not yet men!
And oh, that nasal chocolate milk
Could e'er be sprayed again!

DREAM
By Morgan Greenwald

I walk into a crowded classroom. Kids I've never seen are concentrating on something. The floor is very slanted for some reason, and slippery, I can't walk without hanging on to things. I finally make it to my desk and realize that I'm supposed to be taking a test, and I'm late. I start to panic because when I look at the test I have no idea what it's about, the questions are just written in gibberish. All of a sudden a boy puts a huge lizard under a girl's desk and she starts to scream. The whole room just stares at her like she's crazy, they can't see it. I'm the only other person who can see it. I want to tell her I see it, and that we should poke it with a pencil to get it to move, but when I open my mouth, no sound comes out. The lizard crawls up on her desk and starts very slowly chewing her test.

All of a sudden I'm in the cafeteria. It looks like the food court at the mall we go to in Trumbull, Connecticut, though. Everyone is lining up to get pizza, but I want fried chicken. A boy with red hair tells me the pizza is the only thing you can be sure isn't poisoned by terrorists. Then he laughs and some sort of weird green smoke comes out of his nose and floats in the air like ectoplasm. I wake up.

SCREENPLAY
By Fish Koenig

EXT. SCHOOL — MORNING

A mid-block Manhattan brick public school.
Flag hangs limply in the April heat.

INT. SCHOOL — CLASSROOM — SAME

A crowded sixth-grade class is at their
desks, deep into taking a test. Their TEACHER
makes the rounds, 30-ish, attractive, eagle-
eyed, a sweet Long Island whine.

TEACHER fretfully muscles a stuck window.
It's futile.

> TEACHER
>> Gah! Sorry, you guys. I
>> know it's suffocating in
>> here. Try to concentrate—
>> I'll get Arturo in here.

KEVIN, dark strapping twelve-year-old, shoots
hand up.

> KEVIN
>> I bet I can do it, can I do it?

> TEACHER
> No. Work.

Teacher goes to door, sticks head out.

Kevin leans toward his cute neighbor, ZOE.

>   KEVIN
>   (aside to Zoe)
>   I could definitely unstick
>   that.

>   ZOE
>   Shhh! Shut up, Kevin.

They settle down to work.

>   TEACHER (O.S.)
>   Tara? Is Arturo around? We
>   need more of these windows
>   open so bad.

>   KEVIN
>   (whispers to Zoe)
>   I could.

>   KIDS
>   (to Kevin in unison)
>   Shhh!

>   DISSOLVE TO:

INT. CLASSROOM — LATER

CU CLOCK, READING 11:05.

Kids are totally wilted, shifting in seats, but still hard at work. Teacher is stifling yawn, fanning herself, checking clock.

Kevin is feeling devilish. Accidentally on purpose, he drops his PENCIL on the floor.

ANGLE ON PENCIL

Pencil rolls toward Zoe.

> KEVIN
> (with bogus concern)
> Uh-oh. 'Scuse me, Zoe, but I
> must retrieve my pencil.

Zoe tries to ignore him, continues writing. Kevin ducks down to pick up his pencil.

Rising, he clumsily BUMPS Zoe in the elbow of her writing arm, making her make a mark on her test.

Zoe instantly reacts with all the character-istic fury of the smartest girl in class.

> ZOE
> Watch it! You just, like,
> slammed into me! You just
> made me make, like, this huge
> mark on my test! Thanks a
> lot! Look at this! And *stop
> trying to look at my paper*!

Kevin is deadpan, unapologetic.

Teacher attempts to defuse situation.

>   TEACHER
>   Take it easy, take it easy.
>   Relax, you can erase it,
>   Zoe. Not a big deal. It will
>   not affect your grade on
>   this test, I promise you.
>   And watch out for false
>   accusations. We'll discuss
>   it later.

Zoe returns to work, erasing like mad,
glowering.

Kevin exchanges smirk with JASON, his red-
haired acolyte, across the room.

Zoe shoots Kevin a sidelong glare, right-
eously makes a show of working, thinks:

>   ZOE (V.O.)
>   And thanks for the apology,
>   *not*. I can't believe he
>   probably thinks I, like,
>   *like* him. God, do I hate
>   you, Kevin.

Kevin feigns working, thinks:

                    KEVIN (V.O.)
          I can't believe Posada made
          that throwing error...

Jason, across the room, steals a longing
look at Zoe. Thinks:

                    JASON (V.O.)
               (Brando-esque)
          Zo-eeeeee!

INT. CAFETERIA — LATER

Deafening school lunch in progress. Kevin
and Jason are heading for a table carrying
trays of food, mid-conversation.

                    KEVIN
          --Just shoot an arrow in
          its eye and cut the crystal
          off its back.

                    JASON
          I tried that. You gotta
          come over and help me.

They sit and start eating. Jason opens a
half pint of CHOCOLATE MILK.

                    KEVIN
          I will, don't worry.

Zoe and her friends are visible at a nearby table.

> KEVIN (CONT'D)
> Hey, I got such an awesome joke.

Jason swigs his milk, primed for the joke.

> JASON
> Yeaaah?...

> KEVIN
> This guy walks into a shrink's office, and he's *completely naked,* except he's wrapped in Saran Wrap.

> JASON
> What's a shrink?

> KEVIN
> A psychiatrist, idiot.

> JASON
> Oh, right. Yeah?

> KEVIN
> He's completely naked except he's wrapped in Saran Wrap. And he says, "Doc! Doc! What's wrong with me, Doc?"

And the shrink says, "Well,
first of all, *I can clearly
see your nuts!*"

                  JASON
        (doesn't quite get it)
    Huh?

Jason takes another swallow of chocolate milk.

                  KEVIN
        (leans in, clarifies)
    He's in Saran Wrap. "I can
    clearly see your nuts!"

Jason gets it. EXPLODES with laughter,
spraying chocolate milk out of his nose
onto their food.

Kevin and Jason, laughing maniacally, stumble
to the trash, scrape their food into the can.

Other KIDS are gathered, looking on, Zoe
and GIRLFRIEND among them. Kevin and Jason
are Lords of the Laffs, more hijinks.

                  ZOE
        (with obvious pride)
    God. He is SO irritating.

              GIRLFRIEND
    So irritating...

TEEN MAG
By Rosie Ramos

TRESS DISTRESS:
IT'S NOT THE HEAT . . .
IT'S THE HUMIDITY!
(No more classroom frizzies!)

What it REALLY means when he
"drops his pencil"!
(We crack the Boy Code!)

CHEATING IN SCHOOL:
Our survey will shock you!

Lighten up, girlfriend!
HOW TO BEAT
PERFECTIONISM

Shy Guys vs. Fly Guys:
Who luvs you better?
TAKE OUR QUIZ!

OHMIGOD moments:
"HE LAUGHED SO HARD
MILK CAME OUT HIS NOSE!"
(Tell us yours!)

And . . .
BRITNEY,
BRITNEY,
BRITNEY!
(Because she's Britney!)

INSTANT MESSAGE
By Justin Sirk

Fizzykat:
hi

bwaygrrl1010:
hi

Fizzykat:
where r u?????

bwaygrrl1010:
home

Fizzykat:
do you have school were on spring break still

bwaygrrl1010:
aaaaaaaaaaaaaagggghhhhh!!!
:(((((((((((((((((((((
I'm sooooo jelouse!!!!!!!!

Fizzykat:
☺ lol whats up

bwaygrrl1010:
nm

Fizzykat:
r u still frds w / Zoe?

bwaygrrl1010:
yeah sort of
she was so insane today we had
a test and this kid hit her arm and she made a
pencil mark and sh went INSANE!!!!!!!☺

Fizzykat:
who hit her

bwaygrrl1010:
she said he was cheating a kid named Kevin you don't
know him I don't think

Fizzycat:
i dont know him. is he wierd?

bwaygrrl1010:
YES!!!!!!!!!!!!!!!!!!!!!!!!!!!!!!!!

Fizzykat:
□..□..□......
(I just felt like doing that)

bwaygrrl1010:
u r insane

Fizzykat:
☺☺☺☺☺☺☺☺☺☺☺☺☺☺☺

bwaygrrl1010:
have u ever had a drink come out ur nose
at lunch?

Fizzycat:
NOOOOOOOO ohmigod did u??????

bwaygrrl1010:
No but a kid did today

Fizzykat:
!!!!!!!!!!!!!!!??????????

bwaygrrl:
brb

Fizzykat:
k

Fizzykat:
zzzzzzzzzzzzzzzzzz

Fizzykat:
dum dee dum de dummm

Fizzykat:
WHERE R UUUUUU??????

bwaygrrl1010:
gtg bye!

Fizzykat:
k bye c u

COMIC STRIP
By Jazzmyn Rivera

LETTER
By Madeleine Beers

April 20

Dear Gramma and Grampa,

How are you? I am fine. I hope you had a good Easter. I bet Florida is already scorching!

Mom said you really love to hear anything and everything about school, so okay, here's a typical day in my boring sixth-grade life. This morning we had a reading test, I think I did okay on it. One minor distraction was when this kind of bad kid named Kevin dropped his pencil and bumped into this girl named Zoe (probably trying to cheat, knowing him). She went bananas for no reason, for just this little pencil mark on her test. This is what we call an exciting thing for my class, ho hum.

This was lunch today: drinks, chicken nuggets, Santa Fe potato skins, salad if you want one (no), fruit if you want it (yes), dessert (yes). Oh, by the way, the same kid Kevin made this kid Jason laugh so hard at lunch chocolate milk came out his nose. That was good ☺.

Anyway, I wish I had something interesting to say but that's pretty much all for now. Grampa, I hope your kidney stones are better, or gone, or whatever they're supposed to be. I miss you, come to NYC!

Love,
Annie

CROSSWORD
By Gary Beemer

Across
2. redheaded fountain
3. chicken-like shape
7. toss it here
8. lunch is on me
9. angry
12. assessment
13. writing instrument
15. knee-slapper
19. sometimes it's a kiss
20. work surface

Down
1. guffaw
3. nostril home
4. consume
5. ick!
6. lunchroom
9. moo juice
10. let fall
11. gross!
14. she has class
16. spoon and fork combo
17. Jason's crush
18. Mr. Marchetti's nickname

WORD SEARCH
By Gary Beemer

```
R M J L S H R K C L K T N V C
J N G W M N J U L S U U O A H
W C U A A C N M J X S H S Z O
I B R X P D X C Z O U N E L C
B H D E W C M O C K C O S Y O
L I C N E P E A B A U S X G L
T E S T O C H O F S R A A U A
X L P N Q A Z E L D W J M A T
L E L T H O T U S Z F O A E E
C H I C K E N N U G G E T S M
J F D A R H J I P Q U N W V I
P G M I S P P O V H M R L D L
G T A A I I G F K E R A D X K
T U R E Y N Y Q G E K A R U T
S T Z X N G I Q M G V M U V V
```

TEST
KEVIN
PENCIL
ZOE
CAFETERIA
JOKE
JASON
CHOCOLATE MILK
NOSE
CHICKEN NUGGETS
TRASH

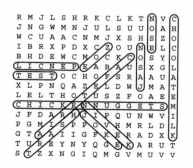

PRESCHOOLER
By Diz Cavallaro

I saw da SCHOOL! I went to school, saw da KIDS! Saw dat big boy dropped da pencil, uh-ohhh, dat boy dropped da PENCIL, and den, and den he bump into da GIRL! And she get MAAAAD. Dat girl is sooo mad. She did a pencil mark. And den, and den, den, we have LUNCH! Me drink appoo joosh. Drink lotta appoo joosh. And da boy have CHOCWAT MILK come out his NOSE! Dat boy have CHOCWAT MILK come out his NOSE!!! hahahahahaha!!....

LEARN TO READ
By Jocelyn Higuchi

Good morning!

It is a good morning.

It is a good morning at school.

See the boys and girls.

They are working.

Work, work, work!

See Zoe.

See Zoe work.

See Jason.

See Jason work.

See Kevin.

Kevin does not work.

Oh! Oh!

Do you see?

See Kevin's pencil drop.

Drop, drop, drop.

Kevin will pick the pencil up.

It is not hard to pick it up.

Oh! Oh!

Kevin bumps Zoe!

Kevin bumps Zoe in the arm.

Poor Zoe!

It made a mark on her work.

Zoe is mad.

Very, very mad.

Zoe says Kevin is bad.

Kevin is not sad.

It is bad that Kevin is not sad.

Now it is time to eat.

The boys and girls eat.

Yum, yum!

The food is good.

See Kevin tell a joke.

It is a funny joke.

Ha, ha!

See Jason laugh.

See Jason's nose.

See milk come out of Jason's nose!

That is funny!

It is very funny to see the milk
come out of Jason's nose!

NEEDS IMPROVEMENT
By Jonathan Fleck-Fishman

The room ful of kids were very quit because there was taking a test that day it was also realy hot. A pencil was droped by a boy named Kevin on the floor. He reatches down to get it and bumped into a girl named Zoes arm. She gets mad at that and says he also cheted! and at him not saying he was even sorry for her making a pensil mark. Later on from then is lunch. A boy with red hair whose named Jason lafed at a joke Kevin told him so hard milk came out his nose on his lunch. they had to throw away the chiken nuggets the milk got on in the trash.

THE TEACHER'S SIDE
By Emily McGee

This heat!

This is crazy, nuts, we've just gotta get some air in here. My God . . . it's not even the end of April!! These poor kids. Never mind the kids, poor ME if these guys don't do well on this stupid test, pleasepleasepleasegod let them do well or I'm in deep, deep guano. Not their fault, not their fault, it was me who spent so much time on that bird unit because we all loved it so much . . . so sue me, New York City! I happen to love teaching more than test-ing, okay????? They'll do fine, I have such faith in these kids, they'll do great, they always do. Jeez, I've just gotta get George to get that corner window unstuck before we all pass out.

Oh my God, look at that Kevin Marchetti, is he a piece of work or what? Dropping his pencil, of COURSE he's the kid who drops his pencil, have they ever done a study on accidentally-on-purpose pencil-dropping as a prime indicator of the alpha male? Whoops, look out, Zoe, he's comin' at ya . . . bingo! Like a singles bar scene, I swear. These kids are tooooo funny. Shhh . . . chill, Zoe . . . not a big deal, Zoe. Attagirl, just erase it . . . let's mooove on. And no, he was NOT cheating, does she think I don't have an iron grip on these things? Eyes in the back of my head? Man, look at that Jason Allen go. Slow down, Jason, what's your hurry, sweetie? Red hair, what is it about redheads? Like a genetic sports car. Vroom. God, I love these kids. I swear, my favorite class ever. I mean yeah, I say that every year, but there really is something special about these guys.

Only 45 more days till freeeedooooom!!! . . . And to think my sister picked working in an office . . . she must be out of her mind!

"George? George, could you please come in and see if you can get that window unstuck? I think it was painted shut . . . in, like 1989 . . ."

BROADWAY MUSICAL
By Rob Bellavance

ACT I
SCENE 1

A SIXTH-GRADE CLASSROOM IN NEW YORK CITY.

> The KIDS are grumpily
> working at their desks on a
> hot morning. Wall clock
> reads 9:40. The TEACHER
> writes the date, April 20,
> and "Reading Test" on the
> blackboard. She freezes as
> the kids sing opening song.

ENSEMBLE KIDS

"A MORNING IN SPRING"

A MORNING IN SPRING
A MORNING IN SPRING
AND OH MY GOSH IT'S HOT AS PEPPER FLAKES!
WE'RE TAKIN' A TEST
WE'RE DOIN' OUR BEST
BUT HEY WE'RE ONLY KIDS FOR HEAVEN SAKES!
WISH WE COULD BE PLAYIN' IN THE PARK SOMEWHERE
'STEAD A' SITTIN' SLAVIN' IN THIS STUPID CHAIR
HURRY SUMMER CAN'CHA HEAR US SING...
THAT WE'RE WASTING A MORNING,
OH WHAT A MORNING,
A BEAUTIFUL MORNING IN SPRING!

                    Music continues as TEACHER
                    struggles to open a window.

          TEACHER
Darn it all! Sorry, children.
Jeepers, it's so darn hot in here, I
bet you're having trouble
concentrating! Maybe I should get the
custodian in here to open this stuck
window.

                    KEVIN (husky handsome boy)
                    shoots hand up.

          KEVIN
I'll try! Can I try?

          TEACHER
          (affectionately scolding)
NO, Kevin. Get back to work on that
test, pronto!

                    Teacher freezes in finger-
                    wagging posture as KIDS
                    reprise song, big finish.

          ENSEMBLE KIDS

HURRY SUMMER CAN'TCHA HEAR US SIIIING...
THAT WE'RE WASTING A MORNING,
OH WHAT A MORNING,
A BEAUTIFUL MORNING IN SPRIIIIIING!

ALL turn back to work,
gripping pencils, and
freeze. Music tick-tocks
as the hands on the wall
clock move from 9:40 to
11:05. As time passes, ALL
slowly droop in their
seats from the hard work
and the heat. Even the
teacher looks wilted.
Music stops.

SPOTLIGHT on Kevin as he
unfreezes to address
audience.

KEVIN
        (to audience)
Have you ever felt like you just
had to DO something? Anything at
all? Just to change things? Because
change is...good?

He turns to speak to the
frozen Zoe, who remains
unresponsive.

KEVIN (cont'd)
Have you ever felt that way, Zoe?
Zoe Blass, who thinks I like her?
And I really don't?

                    Addresses audience again.
                    He raises his pencil high,
                    devilishly poised to drop
                    it, still in spotlight.

          KEVIN (cont'd)
          (triumphantly to audience)
Time for the ooooold pencil drop!

                    He ceremoniously drops
                    pencil towards Zoe's desk.
                    Drum RIMSHOT when it hits
                    the floor. All unfreeze
                    and look toward the sound.
                    Kevin makes a big show of
                    stooping down to retrieve
                    it. Zoe shoots Kevin a
                    little glare.

          KEVIN (cont'd)
          (to Zoe, sarcastically)
I'm sorry, Zoe. I seem to have
dropped my pencil.

                    As Kevin grabs his pencil
                    and rises, he bumps Zoe's
                    writing arm hard. She
                    blows up at him.

          ZOE
Watch it! Look what you just made
me do! Look at this big mark on my

paper! Look at it! And I bet you
were trying to *cheat*!

        Teacher tries to soothe Zoe.

        TEACHER
Calm down, Zoe. It'll erase just
fine. I promise you, it will not
affect your grade. It doesn't have
to look perfect.

        ZOE
But it was perfect! I *want* it to be
perfect!

        TEACHER
Just get back to work everybody. That
means *you,* Kevin Marchetti...and
keep your eyes on your own work!

                Kids all turn back to
                their tests. MUSIC up as
                Zoe sings plaintively in
                spotlight, her rising
                anger directed at the
                oblivious Kevin as the
                song progresses.

ZOE

"I'D BE PERFECT (IF IT WEREN'T FOR YOU)"

YES EVERYBODY KNOWS THAT BARBRA
STREISAND SAID IT BEST:
'PEOPLE WHO NEED PEOPLE' ARE SO
LUCKY AND SO BLESSED
BUT THERE'S ONE THING I ALSO KNOW IS TRUE...
STUPID PEOPLE ALWAYS MESS UP WHAT I DOOOO...!

I'D BE PERFECT IF IT WEREN'T FOR YOU
LIFE WOULD BE A BOWL OF SWEET AND PERFECT
  PEACHES
AT MY DESK ALL CUTE AND CLEAN
I'D LOOK LIKE A MAGAZINE
AS I SOAK UP EVERY WORD THE TEACHER TEACHES

I'D BE PERFECT IF IT WEREN'T FOR YOU
CERTAIN PEOPLE ARE DETERMINED TO BE MORONS
CERTAIN PEOPLE I DESPISE
WHO WILL NOT APOLOGIZE!
WHO JUST BUMP INTO A GIRL AND
DO NOT CARE IF THAT GIRL CRIES!
THEY MAY THINK IT'S JUST A PENCIL MARK
BUT THEY DON'T REALIZE
I'D BE PERFECT...
OH SO PERFECT...
I'D BE PERFECT...
IF IT WEREN'T
FOR
YOOOOOU...!

Zoe gets back to work, martyred. Spotlight on JASON, a red-haired squirt in another row, who looks longingly toward Zoe, unnoticed by the others.

          JASON
          (lovesick wail)
Zo-eeeeeee!!! I love yoooou!!!

                              BLACKOUT.

          SCENE 2

Classroom wall has revolved, revealing the school cafeteria. Kids are horsing around, talking, eating. Kevin and Jason are carrying lunch trays, heading to a table to sit. Zoe and her GIRLFRIENDS are at a table nearby.

          KEVIN
          (to Jason)
You've just gotta work on your fastball.

                    JASON
          Yeah, I know I know...

                    KEVIN
          I'll show you a trick, mine burns now.

                    JASON
          Great! Thanks, Kevin!

                              They sit and start eating.
                              Jason opens a carton of
                              chocolate milk and takes
                              a swig.

                    KEVIN
          Hey, I got a great joke.

                    JASON
          Yeaahhh?

                              Jason leans in, ready for
                              the joke.

                    KEVIN
          It's really funny. I mean really,
          really funny.

                              The general cafeteria
                              hubbub STOPS. KIDS around
                              them lean in theatrically.
                              MUSIC sting.

                    JASON
Yeaahhh????

                    KEVIN
I'm talkin' really, really, REALLY
funny.

                         Music sting. Kids speak in
                         unison, captivated.

                    JASON AND KIDS
Yeaahhh????

                         Kevin makes a big show of
                         whispering the joke into
                         eager Jason's ear. There's
                         a suspenseful beat...
                         Jason remains clueless.

                    JASON
I don't get it.

                         Music WHOMPS. Slightly
                         exasperated Kevin whispers
                         broadly again, clarifying
                         punch line. Music UP. Kids
                         lean in, Jason takes
                         another big gulp of milk.
                         We see the punch line
                         register broadly in
                         Jason's face...he cracks

                        up and sprays milk
                        violently, all over their
                        lunches.

          KEVIN
          (laughing/disgusted)
Ewww! My chicken nuggets!!! You
sprayed milk out your NOSE!...

                        Kevin and Jason are
                        laughing like hyenas as
                        kids around them are in a
                        joyful uproar. Nearby ZOE
                        is at the front, pointing
                        in disgust.

          ZOE
Aaagh! He squirted milk out of his
nose!!

          KID 1
          (gleefully)
Milk out the nose! Yes, indeeeed! The
ol' milk-out-the-nose laugh!

          KID 2
Milk out the noooose!!!!...

                        MUSIC up, kids sing and
                        dance big number all over
                        the cafeteria.

ENSEMBLE KIDS

"MILK OUT THE NOSE"

THERE'S ALL KINDS A' FUNNY
AND ALL KINDS A' JOKES
THERE'S BELLY LAUGHS AND CHUCKLES
AND LAUGHIN' TIL YA CHOKE
BUT HOPE YOU'RE FAMILIAR
WITH THE GREATEST OF THOSE
"HOW FUNNY IS IT??"
MILK OUT THE NOSE!

(CHORUS)

MILK OUT THE NOSE!
MILK OUT THE NOSE!
THAT'S WHEN YA KNOW THAT YOU'VE GOT 'EM!
MAKE SURE YOUR CHICKEN
NUGGETS ARE SAFE
CUZ THIS KINDA FUNNY WILL SNOT 'EM!
MILK OUT THE NOSE!
MILK OUT THE NOSE!
BACK WHEN THE SCHOOLS WERE JURASSIC
I BETCHA LOTSA YAK MILK
WAS SPRAYIN' THE CAVE!
FOLKS, IT'S A COMEDY CLASSIIIC!

BLACKOUT.

PESSIMIST
By Ben Rizzo

These kids are never gonna be able to do well on this reading test, it's just too insanely hot to concentrate. These April heat waves are always a bad sign, we're probably in for a miserable summer. I can't believe anyone questions the global warming theory, the earth's atmosphere is so obviously screwed up. Too late to do anything about it, might as well just accept we're gonna be charcoal, right?

Look at that big restless boy, what a loser. It's amazing how easy it is to predict what kids will be like when they grow up. He's muscular looking now but I bet he'll be a total lard-ball by the time he's 25. And unemployable, the kid can't sit still—dropping his pencil on purpose, the little cheating scumbag—sure sign he's going nowhere. And the girl sitting next to him, whiny little tattletale, all hysterical about a stupid pencil mark on her test. Actually I bet the testing people DO take off points for neatness, knowing them. But what an incredibly annoying little girl. Hope she ends up with a decent career as somebody's irritating receptionist because marriage is *definitely* not in the cards. . . .

God, the cafeteria noise could practically make your ears bleed. And the food! I wonder if the chicken nuggets and "Santa Fe potato skins" already come frozen with bacteria or if the lunch ladies have to add it. "Cafeteria Worker," talk about a dead-end job, they must be suicidal having to dish out this slop to these brats every day. . . .

Whoa, gross, one kid just laughed so hard milk came out his nose. Somebody should tell him aspirated food can give you a wicked sinus infection. And the sinuses are linked to the brain cavity, so any infection there can be potentially deadly. Not that I'm saying it WILL happen, but it COULD. Stuff happens. You gotta be prepared for the worst.

OPTIMIST
By Jessica Hochstein

This is absolutely my favorite time of year! I mean, winter is great, all white and crisp and beautiful . . . and of course I love summer and fall . . . but when the April flowers are out and the mornings warm up like this . . . heaven!

These kids are doing such a great job concentrating, it's quite amazing how mature kids suddenly are by 6th grade, isn't it? And that big mischievous boy who can't seem to sit still . . . don't you love it?! What a sure sign of a future leader, that kind of restless energy. I wouldn't be surprised if he were running his own company by twenty-five, and running marathons, and a millionaire. I always foresee great things for pencil-droppers ☺! And that girl he bumped, such a perfectionist, wanting so badly to show neat work . . . there's no way her test score would be affected by such a tiny thing, but for her to CARE so much is very rare and admirable. And of course the boy wasn't cheating! I think she's just being a moral watchdog for her peers, scolding him just to keep him on his toes . . . what a great success she'll be someday, in her career and as a wife and mother. She'll be able to do it all, no question!

Is there anyplace in the world as funny and lively as a school cafeteria?? The noise level certainly does wake you up! Boy, these kids are lucky to live in a country where they can take these big delicious lunches for granted. And these cafeteria workers, such great people, many from countries where jobs simply don't exist . . . you can see the pleasure they get from good hard work twinkling in their eyes. I swear, if you want to see the very best of the United States of America, visit a public school cafeteria. It almost makes me cry, it's so full of life and humanity in all its silly, messy, loud, poetic, courageous glory!

Oh, and of course one boy laughed so hard at a joke, milk came out of his nose. Does it get any better than that? Stuff happens! Prepare for the best!

DISINTERESTED PARTY
By Chardinay King

I wasn't there, but supposedly a kid dropped a pencil and hit a girl in the arm.

I guess it made her make some kind of mark on her test and she went nuts. He was cheating, supposedly, or trying to look up her skirt or something.

The cafeteria was apparently just as weird.

Kids were laughing about somebody's drink coming out of their nose, or maybe somebody barfed?

Whatever.

POLITICALLY CORRECT
By Graham Beckwith

It's just unconscionable on a day as hot as this one that there's no air-conditioning in most NYC public schools! Yes, ACs are toxic to the environment, but it seems to me the adverse effect of the heat on the children, particularly the ones with weight challenges, would make it a worthy investment of funds.

The sixth-grade children were taking a "standardized" test today, which is of course still unacceptably biased, both culturally and against the differently abled. And when I consider the externalities, the sheer number of trees slaughtered and chemicals released in the production of the paper used for *this test alone*, I could cry. But that's another issue. The issue that shocked me the most was an incident of physical harassment I witnessed between two students that went virtually unaddressed by the teacher. A boy dropped his pencil on the floor, clearly being intentionally disruptive. As he was picking it up, he deliberately bumped a girl at the neighboring desk in a way that can only be described as an assault. The teacher's gender bias was abundantly clear in the way she made light of the abuse. Even when the girl was obviously distressed, pointing out that the assault had made her make an unsightly mark on her test, and asserting that he'd been trying to cheat, the teacher made light of the incident and the boy went unpunished. I intend to file a complaint against the school on the girl's behalf, to make sure that no female student has to endure such an ordeal again.

I visited the cafeteria to see if there were any health or safety concerns. The food service workers barely make a living wage but the working conditions at this particular school appeared to be up to standards. As for the food, it was typically less than fresh and far too high in fats and carbohydrates but at least minimally nutritious, consisting of "chicken nuggets" and something called "Santa Fe Potato Skins," which, while vaguely offensive to Hispanic and Native Americans, at least appeared to be made of potato. Though barely adequate, alternatives were offered to those with nut allergies, lactose intolerance, and vegetarian diets.

I must report, however, that I overheard the same boy who'd been violent in the classroom telling an extremely offensive, age-inappropriate joke. This is of concern. I feel I have no choice but to recommend that he be evaluated, as there could no doubt be some underlying behavioral or learning disorder contributing to his seemingly chronic puerility.

LABELS
By Stephanie Jones

You know the type, an Academically Excellent, Impressively Diverse Upper West Side Public Middle School with an Involved Parent Body, more Banana Republic at the PTA than Prada. Hot April morning, kids filing in with their Sony Discmen and iPod Minis dangling from the ubiquitous Jansports, girls in their Reef and Steve Madden sandals, Pumas, Juicy tees, jeans from anywhere but Mavi preferred. Boys in their Quicksilver, Plugg cargos, Nikes, some Ecko, Sean John, but this is a school where labels don't matter.

The sixth graders are taking your basic Citywide Reading Test. Overworked Underpaid Teacher stands watch, Single, Long Island Jewish, thirtyish, clothes from H&M, Express for weekends. Heavyset future Romeo drops his pencil in a patented Smooth Move to annoy the Princess at the Desk Next Door. Getting up, he gives her the ol' Accidental Bump, possibly attempting the Casual Cheat, she goes Postal, classic case of Love/Hate but they're still Tweens and don't really know that yet. Redheaded standard-issue Lovesick Sidekick watches from across the room.

Typical Cafeteria Madness follows. The traditional Unidentifiable Breaded, Frozen Institutional Fare is heated and dished up by Disgruntled Plastic-Capped Lunch Ladies. Romeo tells Mildly Dirty Joke Involving Male Genitalia to Sidekick, who performs classic Patented Sitcom Spit-Take with bonus Drink-out-the-Nose.

EXCLAMATORY
By Marina Kolodzyn

Who would believe it could be this hot! In April! And so many kids crammed into the room! Taking a reading test, of all things! Then this boy dropped his pencil on purpose! Just because he was bored, if you can believe it! And as he picked it up, he bumped the girl next to him! In her writing arm, of all places! It made her make a mark on her paper! She was furious, as you can well imagine! Accused him of, get this, CHEATING! And if that weren't enough, he didn't even apologize!

Later on, the cafeteria was a madhouse! The boy who bumped the girl was at it again! This time he told a joke that was a little dirty, of course! And this other boy laughed so hard milk came out of his nose! You should have seen it! It was hysterical!

PICTURE ONLY
By Dakota Falk

[A dingy, stained, pale-blue classroom with dark wood-work. Children sit at desks, approximately eleven years old, multiracial, wearing colorful casual clothing. They appear to be sweaty and restless. There is a female teacher, thirtyish, dark-haired, stylishly dressed in a sleeveless black shirt, blue denim skirt, and black sandals. She appears to be watching the children as they are writing on paper with pencils. A large dark-haired boy in a Houston Astros T-shirt and baggy black basketball shorts jiggles his knee up and down and drops his pencil. He bends to pick it up and appears to hit the arm of the girl sitting next to him as he rises. She has very long dark brown hair and wears a pale pink T-shirt with the word 'happy' written in dark pink script, tight capri-length jeans, and purple platform sandals. She appears to be furious at the boy who bumped her, and keeps gesturing wildly at the paper in front of her. The teacher approaches and appears to scold them, makes calming motions with her hands. The boy stares down at his paper and smirks slightly. The girl glares.]

[A gray-painted cafeteria with a painted mural of large flowers, swarming with children lined up to be served food and hurrying with brown trays to gray formica folding tables. The boy who bumped the girl is sitting at a table across from a smaller red-haired boy who is drinking from a carton and eating what appear to be small pieces of breaded chicken. The larger boy has a devilish smile on his face and looks around furtively as he leans in to speak to the red-haired boy. Suddenly the red-haired boy explodes with laughter, spraying his drink through his nose, all over his food. Everyone in the vicinity looks on with disgust and laughter. The boys jump up from the table and with much back-slapping and horseplay head to a large black metal trash barrel and scrape their food into it.]

SOUND ONLY
By Jeff Reese

[Woman talking.]
[Chairs scraping.]
[Papers rustling. Coughing. Pencils scratching.]
[Clock ticking.]
[Sighing. Tapping.]
[Plink!]
[Boy talking. Girl yelling. Woman scolding.]
[Eraser rubbing. Grumbling.]

[Plastic clattering, metal clinking.]
[Deafening screaming, laughing, chatter.]
[Food munching, swallowing. Drink gulping.]
[Boys talking. Boy laughing. Nose snorting.]
[Kids hysterical.]
[Can banging. Plastic scraping.]

CROSS-EXAMINATION
By Danielle Nesby

Q: Exactly where did this happen?
A: A sixth-grade classroom.

Q: And how do you know it was the sixth grade, and not the seventh or even the fifth?
A: It's my classroom and I'm in the sixth.

Q: How many children were involved?
A: Twenty-something. Plus a teacher.

Q: Twenty-two? Twenty-eight?
A: Probably more like twenty-eight.

Q: Did you notice anything strange in particular? Anything at all?
A: Strange?

Q: Strange behavior, perhaps?
A: Well, Kevin seemed very restless.

Q: Let the record show the witness is indicating Mr. Marchetti. So, Mr. Marchetti seemed very restless, you say. And how did you draw this conclusion?
A: He kept jiggling his leg and tapping his pencil like he was, y'know, restless.

Q: I see. And this was what you would call "strange behavior"...?
A: Well, you said did I notice anything at all—

Q:—stranger than the behavior that followed? The girl's behavior?
A: That was kinda strange, too.

Q: Would you tell us precisely what happened, please, in your own words.

A: Sure. Um . . . Kevin was acting restless, and then he dropped his pencil on purpose.

Q: And what made you think that he dropped his pencil on purpose?

A: I dunno. He just seemed like he wanted to get everybody's attention.

Q: "Seemed." I see. So in your opinion, Mr. Marchetti simply enjoys attention?

A: Yeah. Yes, I would say that. And he enjoyed making the girl mad.

Q: Did Mr. Marchetti say anything that would make you think he enjoyed making the girl mad?

A: Noooo, but . . . he was kinda smiling . . .

Q: Could he, in fact, have felt very badly about the dropped pencil, very badly indeed? And might he have been smiling about something else entirely at that moment?

A: Well, yeah, I guess that's possible.

Q: And who was this girl?

A: Zoe, the girl sitting next to him. She got furious because he bumped her arm when he picked up his pencil.

Q: Did he injure the girl?

A: No, not really . . . but he made her make a mark on the test we were taking, and she said he was trying to cheat.

Q: This was merely her opinion, correct?

A: Yeah. Correct.

Q: Would you say the girl's reaction was extreme?
A: Um . . . maybe a little . . .

Q: Overly emotional?
A: Maybe. Yeah, definitely . . .

Q: Inappropriately intense? Violent?
(Lawyer: Objection! Leading the witness . . .)
(Judge: Sustained. Please continue.)
Q: How did the incident resolve?
A: The teacher calmed her down.

Q: Which was no doubt quite difficult to do, as hysterical as the girl was . . . ?
(Lawyer: Objection!)
(Judge: Sustained.)
Q: Did you then witness Mr. Marchetti's demeanor in the lunchroom?
A: Demeanor?

Q: His behavior, his mood?
A: Yeah, I witnessed him having a very funny demeanor.

Q: Funny amusing, or funny peculiar?
A: Funny amusing. He told a redheaded kid a joke that made him laugh milk out of his nose.

Q: Were there other witnesses to this?
A: Tons. They had to throw chicken nuggets away that had nose milk on them.

Q: And how do you know they threw their lunches away because they had nose milk on them?
A: I just figured that was why. . . .

Q: Isn't it possible that they threw those chicken nuggets away NOT because of nose milk, indeed NOT because of anything Mr. Marchetti said or did, but because the chicken nuggets simply TASTED BAD, as they do EVERY time they are served?
A: I . . . I guess that's possible.

Q: Thank you. That will be all.

PSYCHIC
By Buddy Corsa

Let me just . . . tune in for a moment, see what They feel like telling me . . . my guides on the Other Side, Queen Celestina and Larry . . . sometimes They're occasionally out. . . or cranky . . . or screening their calls . . .

[Pause]

Hmm. This is interesting. I'm getting school, images of a class-room. Does that make sense to you? Have you ever been in a school, or a classroom of any kind at all? . . . Oh, really! . . . Yes, They are uncannily perceptive. Now let me seeee . . .

[Pause]

This classroom is . . . well, I'm feeling it's hot. They're telling me it's uncomfortable. They're saying it's hard to concentrate. That's exactly what They're saying: "It's hard to concentrate!" [laughs], which at first I thought was one of Their little jokes—They do that. I thought They were saying They're having trouble concentrating [laughs]. They're just such cutups on the Other Side, they really are.

[Pause]

Hmm. I'm getting something . . . sharp. Well, maybe not sharp, but . . . pointy. A spear? No, smaller . . . a knitting needle? Does that mean anything to you? A knitting needle dropping on the floor? It's not entirely clear. Give it some thought—sometimes these things make sense later.

[Pause]

Oh my. I'm feeling anger in here, in my chest. I'm seeing a girl, a very angry girl. Something about a boy, and the knitting needle. Did

133

a boy stab a girl with a knitting needle when you were in school? I know it sounds odd, but this girl is just so, so upset. I'm not feeling she was that badly hurt, though . . . I'm getting a Z. Her name starts with Z. A Zelda? A Zoe? . . .

[Pause]

This sounds silly, but They're laughing so hard I can hardly understand what They're saying. . . .

[Pause]

Did you, maybe, squirt chocolate milk out of your nose or something? Does that make any sense? Because I'm getting a nose, and chocolate milk . . .

HORROR
By Steven Spivack

Tick.

Tick.

Tick.

The clock itself seemed a little tentative, a bit nervous to find itself in this airless classroom, its walls the color of . . .

A diseased pigeon, Jason said to himself. Or perhaps the gray-blue of a preserved brain, floating listlessly in formaldehyde. Yeah, that was it. A dead brain. Just like his.

Man, it was hot.

Jason stole a glance at Zoe across the room and felt his heart stir to life for one quick instant. Zoe Blass, his unwitting prey. Zoe, his soul mate, the center of his universe, who would finally see him, finally love him, today!

He must concentrate.

He must not make a mistake.

He had turned the fantasy over and over in his mind's eye for weeks, the way a man would plot a murder. Only this would not be murder. This would be another kind of death.

The death of his old, invisible self.

Jason had a secret. Jason could move things. Change things. With his mind. When he was three or four, his mother noticed things that she dared not mention, afraid people would think she was going crazy. The first time, he made a mini marshmallow roll across a table when she said he couldn't have one. She saw it with her own eyes. He just giggled, as though it was nothing. And from there, it continued.

Birthday candles extinguished without a breath.

Slinkys climbing *up* the stairs.

When he turned six, she begged him to stop. She was too frightened of his power. And to be honest, so was Jason. It was hard enough to be a skinny red-haired shrimp without being a telekinetic freak, too. So it became his secret.

Tick.

Tick.

Tick.

Kevin Marchetti yawned loudly.

Scribble.

Scribble.

Sigh.

The class worked diligently on their reading tests. Silly little robots. Only Zoe deserved him.

11:02. My God, she looked beautiful in her little pink shirt that said HAPPY. But soon he would have to give her something to be unhappy about. Very unhappy.

Kevin jiggled his leg. A good sign—he was already restless. This would be easy.

Too easy.

Now, Jason thought. *Now.*

He turned his gaze to Kevin and shaded his eyes with his hand. No one could see them as his pupils glowed a hellish red, burning like an invisible laser into Kevin's unsuspecting pea brain.

Kevin's jaw dropped slack in a brief, comatose state that could easily be mistaken for simple boredom. His knee jiggled almost spastically, and he tapped his pencil on his desk like a demonic one-armed drummer.

More, urged Jason. *Give me more, Kevin.* He concentrated harder on the pencil, scowling it into submission with every red cell of his being, sweat beading on his forehead. It was one thing to move small objects, quite another to actually break a human being's grasp.

But he did it. Kevin raised his arm like a zombie and let the pencil drop, shattering the silence, just as Jason had foreseen it, willed it.

All heads turned at the sound, mouths agape. The pencil rolled to a stop right beside Zoe's feet. (Platform shoes. Purple.)

Kevin looked a bit baffled. A puppet with an unseen master. But he relished the excuse to disturb Zoe, so he bent down to get the pencil under her desk.

"Excuse me, Zoe," he said, all artificial sweetener. "I must retrieve my pencil."

Zoe was annoyed but ignored him. *Attagirl,* thought Jason. *Ignore him or hate his guts— those are the two things I'll allow.*

And now for the grand finale. As Kevin got up with his pencil, Jason focused his powers with every shred of his being.

Why did no one else notice the walls begin to heave, in and out, like gasping lungs? How was it possible they didn't hear the wind rising in the room, whistling at first, then howling like a rabid wolf? In Jason's mind's eye the books and papers flew, the windows rattled in their frames. The kids clung to their desks like dories thrashed by waves, staring about them in terror as Jason stood on his desk like a captain on the deck of a rocking, groaning ghost ship. He pointed at Kevin and unleashed a bolt of force so strong, Kevin's body jerked like a huge fish on a straining line. With the lift of a finger, Jason sent him crashing into Zoe's writing arm and into a special nightmare of his making: Zoe's wrath.

Kevin was dead meat.

All Jason had to do now was watch and enjoy.

"My test!" she screamed, her mouth a horrifying mask of anger. "You made me make a mark on my test! A maaark! On my teeeest! And you were trying to cheat!"

Her hatred of Kevin reached new heights of raw fury. This was better than Jason had even imagined. The end of Zoe's and Kevin's sixth-grade love/hate thing was in sight. And he had ended it.

Ms. Petricoff hurried over to calm things down, but Jason's joy was so overwhelming he hardly listened, hardly saw. He roused himself from the mist of his happiness only to catch Zoe's eye, just for an instant, and give her a sympathetic wink. He was almost positive she saw it. And he was almost certain she looked grateful.

The day drifted into lunch. Jason couldn't wait to sit near Zoe, maybe even say something nice about the test incident. But Kevin buddied up to him as he headed for a table, and sat down across from him. Jason could see Zoe and her friends at a table nearby.

"Hey, I got a good joke," Kevin mumbled through a mouthful of chicken nuggets.

Jason took a big swig of his chocolate milk and tried not to look at Zoe too obviously.

"Yeah?"

Kevin looked around furtively and opted to whisper it into Jason's ear.

Zoe was watching them. Watching him, Jason— he was sure of it. He tried to look cool and popular as he listened to Kevin's lame joke.

"Yeah?" he said expectantly. He raised the milk carton to his lips, took another gulp.

Kevin leaned in to whisper the punch line.

The rest was a blur of chocolate milk and hysteria. It was a funny joke. Screams and cries of "Ohmigod" and "Ewwww!" punctuated the air as milk snorted out of Jason's nose and all over their food. And as he flailed, drowning in a fresh wave of geekdom, he saw Zoe's face looming above the crowd, looking at . . . Kevin. With something like love.

He had lost. Again.

And in his mind's eye, he stood on the table, the Dark Lord of the Lunchroom, pointing his finger and narrowing his blood-red gaze . . .

BAD TRANSLATION
By Yun Li

The hotness of the room is very uncomfortable on this day for the many children having eleven years. They are executing a test. The boy Kevin Marchetti is having much boredom and trouble-making! To the floor his pencil is descended, and makes to roll below the desk of the girl named Zoe. Kevin is going down to be getting it, when at this moment—ouf!—the girl is hit very strong by Kevin. She is very angry for this hit for the reason of making the pencil error on her test! And there is an accusation of improper looking at her paper!

Later, we are in the Dining Hall which is very, extra loud. The children are seating at the tables of food, such as chicken pieces and the potato peels of the Spanish. The boy Kevin is telling a story which is humorous to the boy Jason, and the boy Jason makes the drink of milk come out of his nose by laughing! They are having to dispose of the chicken pieces in the waste container!

INSTRUCTIONS
By Sandra Bruce

Congratulations on the purchase of your SIXTH-GRADE SHENANIGANS™ MILK OUT THE NOSE! kit! Ready to start? Have fun!

You will need:

1 classroom
1 cafeteria
28 children (11 and 12 years, assorted sizes)
1 teacher

Enclosed items:

Pencils (28)
Test booklets (28)
Chicken nuggets (16)
Chocolate milk container (1)

Step 1:

Preheat classroom to 93 degrees. Fill with children. Insert teacher.

Step 2:

Place enclosed pencils and test booklets on desks. Watch children work! (Note: Children will be drowsy. This is normal.)

Step 3:
Let children sit undisturbed 30–35 minutes or until knee of largest boy begins jiggling vigorously. Pencil of largest boy will then drop to floor.

Step 4:
Allow largest boy to pick up pencil. When he sits up, he will strike arm of small girl seated next to him and her pencil will scratch across her test. WATCH WHAT HAPPENS!

Step 5:
Move children to cafeteria. (Caution: CHILDREN WILL BE LOUD. Adjust volume as necessary.)

Step 6:
Divide enclosed chicken nuggets onto 2 plastic plates (plates, cutlery, and additional food not included). Seat largest boy across from red-haired boy.

Step 7:
Place enclosed chocolate milk container in hand of red-haired boy. Largest boy will begin telling a joke!

Step 8:
Sit back and watch the wacky result!!!

(Note: It is very important that the red-haired boy takes a gulp of milk at the precise moment the largest boy tells "punch line." If largest boy finishes joke and red-haired boy laughs without performing expected squirting action from nose, repeat steps 5–7.)

Enjoy these crazy SHENANIGANS™ again and again!

More kits available from
SIXTH-GRADE SHENANIGANS™:

SLEEPLESS SLEEPOVER!
PUBLIC SCREAMING!
UNBELIEVABLY EMBARRASSING MOM!
ZIT SNIT!
SKATEBOARD MENACE!

FROM A DISTANCE
By A.J. Conway

It's some kind of indoor gathering. People are sitting in rows. There's very little movement. Then someone moves away from their seat and back again, causing some sort of disturbance. I think I hear yelling. Later, there's another large room full of people, racing around and carrying things. Some are seated at tables. There's a faint smell of food. There's another disturbance of some kind, and then what sounds like laughter.

METAPHORICAL
By Milo Korzienowsky

The classroom was like warm Jell-O: hopeful for cool, begging for bounce, young. Today, even the kids' mother hen of a teacher was thinking she'd rather be anywhere but this particular coop.

Kevin Marchetti sat working on his test, jiggling his knee like a teakettle at the boil. A low-whistling, restless teakettle. His dropped pencil went off like a small pipe bomb in the quiet. No injuries, just a statement.

Kevin folded his big self under his desk like bad origami. His hand spidered across the aisle to the walled fortress of Her Highness Zoe Blass and retrieved his pencil from under her desk with an apology as hollow as a can of nothin'.

"I'm terribly sorry, I seem to have dropped my pencil," he oozed like hair product. Zoe's look was frozen worms.

Kevin popped up like a demented jack-in-the-box and bumped Zoe's toothpick arm with roller-rink gusto. Her pencil gouged a zig across the face of her test like Zorro in a bad mood.

"Look what you made me dooooo!" she screamed, Mental Case Barbie. "You made me make this huge mark on my teeest!! And you were *cheating*!!"

Even Mother Hen's reassurances couldn't douse the fireworks of Zoe's freak-out. Being 11 is a dogsled ride through a cat factory.

She finally settled down like a volcano with a grudge. And lovesick Jason gave her a look like a feather blown across the room.

Later, the cafeteria noise was enough to make your ears quit. In the simple act of getting food and sitting, the girls were screaming like Beatles fans and the boys were stuck in some kind of pinball machine of nonstop hitting and flinging. Kevin and Jason sat like chained monkeys with little jigsaw puzzles of mysterious food shapes on their plates.

"I got a good joke," said Kevin with jailbird conspiracy. Jason raised his chocolate milk to his mouth and tossed it down like a flyweight boxer between rounds.

"Yeah?" Jason said, taking another gulp of chocolate milk, an arrow tight at the bow.

Kevin told it. Jason cracked up. The arrow flew, straight out of his nose.

BLANK VERSE
by Thai Wheeler

I saw it
f
a
l
l
(the pencil, that is)
like an axe
smiting calm.
I was bothered
but not as much
as the girl.
I heard it told
(the lunchroom joke)
and was amused.
But not as much
as the red-haired boy.
The red-haired boy was
u   n   d   o   n   e !
The red-haired boy
was better than the joke.
He was laughing
until chocolate milk
came out of his nose.
He was the best
today
had to offer.

KEVIN'S SIDE
By Seb Harris

Hi, I'm Kevin Marchetti and these are my own words.
Ummm . . . yeah.
Hot room, reading test, fruit bowl fruit bowl bla bla blaaaa.
I'm twelve.
I'm sitting with my leg wiggling.
I'm sitting like the *Challenger* countdown.
I'm sitting like a cigar on the *Hindenburg*.
I'm sitting like the dessert cart on the *Titanic*.
Hey, nothing looks tragic until it is. Right?
Coffee and doughnuts at the World Trade Center.

(Oh, I'm sorry. Is it too mean to say the World Trade Center? Are we not ready for that?)

In case you're wondering, I dropped my pencil on purpose. And I hit Zoe's arm on purpose when I picked it up. So she'd be mad. So I'd be the person she was thinking of, at the moment that I wanted her to think of me.

And in case you're wondering, I was cheating.
Yes.
I was actually cheating. Okay? Mystery solved.

So Ms. Petricoff would be mad. So my mom would be mad. So I'd be the person they were thinking of, at the moment that I wanted them to think of me. But Ms. Petricoff gave me the benefit of the doubt. Because she wants me to like her. So I'll Open Up. So she can feel good about that.

I told a joke in the cafeteria. I always tell the best ones. I made Jason laugh so hard chocolate milk squirted out of his nose.

In case you're wondering, I don't laugh or cry as hard as other people.

I make things happen so things won't happen to me.

It's a full-time job. But I'm job hunting.

Betcha didn't think li'l Kevin would be so insightful. Whoot!

SONNET
By Pearl Richardson

The docile children harnessed to their test,
All clueless to the reason and the rhyme;
Each Beauty and each Beast and hopeful Pest,
Are yoked as one in Spring's bright golden time.
Here restless heart and tooth-worn pencil slipp'd,
And boy and rosy elbow did collide;
And all did gape as that fair maiden flipp'd,
But all is rendered mist by time and tide.
As jonquils bloom and larks reprise their song,
As clouds do rain and spiders spin their silk,
The song of red-haired laughter is ne'er wrong;
Nor chicken spoiled by noses snorting milk!
In Love's sweet groaning school we all do live
And work, and play, and laugh, and pray forgive.

THE CHICKEN NUGGET'S SIDE
By Anonymous

Nugget bored.

Brr. Cold. Freezer.

Lunch lady. Evil lunch lady rubber hands.

Rip bag, dump nuggets on metal.

Metal hot. Metal very, very hot. Red all around. Nugget hot.

Spatula.

Ahhh. Plate.

Plate with Santa Fe potato skins. Know them. Friends. Good.

Boy carry nuggets to table. Big boy. Will feed big boy. Proud.

Big boy funny. Other boy laugh.

Nooooo!! NOOOOOOOO!!!!

Chocolate milk. Nose. Nugget wet. Nugget non-crispy.

Trash.

Dark.

Potato skins cry.

Nugget not cry.

Nugget brave.

Nugget see light at top of trash.

Nugget hope.

Do not feel bad for nugget.

Nugget has no brain.

Nugget has no nervous system.

Nugget inanimate object.

Anonymous just think fun to include nugget in book.

Here's a list of things that happened between the Fruit Bowl Project and graduation:

> Gary Beemer, Yun Li, Max Baum-White, and Danielle Nesby got into Stuyvesant High School. Jonathan Fleck-Fishman did not. His parents are investigating.

> Chardinay King lost twenty-seven pounds and sang Christina Aguilera's "Beautiful" in the Spring Revue.

> Pearl Richardson and Steven Spivack are not sure if they actually like each other or just both love Lou Reed, but they hang out.

> Rob Bellavance is enrolled at soccer camp *and* Summerstage theater camp. His father is outwardly supportive.

> Mia McCabe-Alvarez got into Phillips Exeter Academy on a full scholarship but turned it down to stay in the Bronx.

Seb Harris and Sandra Bruce made out on the bus on the class trip to Frost Valley.

Jawshua Perry and Emily McGee made out on the way back.

Stephanie Jones and Jenna Bromberg are still not, and will never be, friends.

Nick Thompson showed the Fruit Bowl project to a publisher. We'll see what happens.

About the Author

Sarah Durkee has been an Emmy-winning children's television songwriter and scriptwriter, a children's author, a rock lyricist, a playwright, a poet, and a comedy writer. This is her first novel, and the first time she's been able to be all of them simultaneously.